"I can't decide whether you're afraid of me or yourself,"

Joe whispered as he stepped up behind her.

He was so close, Rachel could feel his breath in her hair. "I'm not afraid of anything."

He caressed her back. "Why are you so tense?"

"I'm not tense." How could he think she was tense when every bone in her body seemed to dissolve at his touch?

He lifted her hair and nibbled the back of her neck. "When are you going to stop fighting it and admit that there's something between us?"

She wanted to wrench away from him, but his warm lips sent a delightful shiver down her spine. "Never."

"Never say never," Joe whispered....

Dear Reader,

At Silhouette Romance we're celebrating the start of 1994 with a wonderful lineup of exciting love stories. Get set for a year filled with terrific books by the authors you love best, and brand-new names you'll be delighted to discover.

Those FABULOUS FATHERS continue, with Linc Rider in Kristin Morgan's *Rebel Dad*. Linc was a mysterious drifter who entered the lives of widowed Jillian Fontenot and her adopted son. Little did Jillian know he was a father in search of a child—*her* child.

Pepper Adams is back with *Lady Willpower*. In this charming battle of wills, Mayor Joe Morgan meets his match when Rachel Fox comes to his town and changes it—and Joe!

It's a story of love lost and found in Marie Ferrarella's *Aunt Connie's Wedding*. Carole Anne Wellsley was home for her aunt's wedding, and Dr. Jefferson Drumm wasn't letting her get away again!

And don't miss Rebecca Daniels's *Loving the Enemy*. This popular Intimate Moments author brings her special brand of passion to the Silhouette Romance line. Rounding out the month, look for books by Geeta Kingsley and Jude Randal.

We hope that you'll be joining us in the coming months for books by Diana Palmer, Elizabeth August, Suzanne Carey and many more of your favorite authors.

Anne Canadeo
Senior Editor

Please address questions and book requests to:
Reader Service
U.S.: P.O. Box 1325, Buffalo, NY 14269
Canadian: P.O. Box 1050, Niagara Falls, Ont. L2E 7G7

LADY WILLPOWER
Pepper Adams

Silhouette
ROMANCE™
Published by Silhouette Books
America's Publisher of Contemporary Romance

This book is dedicated to our husbands and children.
Thank you for your patience and tolerance over the
years. It's not easy having a writer in the house.

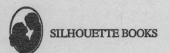 SILHOUETTE BOOKS

ISBN 0-373-08983-X

LADY WILLPOWER

Copyright © 1994 by Debrah Morris and Pat Shaver

This edition published by arrangement with Harlequin Enterprises B.V.

Printed in U.S.A.

Books by Pepper Adams

Silhouette Romance

Heavenly Bodies #486
In Hot Pursuit #504
Taking Savanah #600
*Cimarron Knight #724
*Cimarron Glory #740
*Cimarron Rebel #753
Hunter At Large #805
That Old Black Magic #842
Rookie Dad #862
Wake Up Little Susie #897
Mad About Maggie #964
Lady Willpower #983

*Cimarron Stories

PEPPER ADAMS

is the pseudonym of Debrah Morris and Pat Shaver, who have co-authored over twenty romances. They live in Norman, Oklahoma, and both are married with children. When they started working together, they made a pact. They vowed to give writing up if it ever stopped being fun. That was in 1984, and they see no end in sight. Their humorous, uplifting stories reflect their continuing love for the genre and their belief in the power of love.

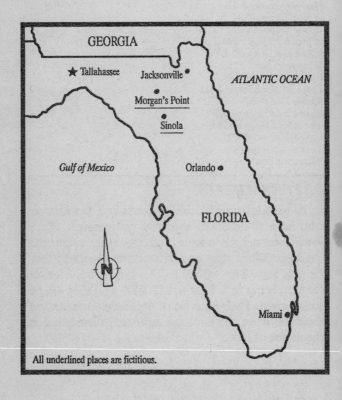

All underlined places are fictitious.

Chapter One

"I can't tell a weed from a begonia, Mom. You'll have to point them out." Rachel Fox swatted at a buzzing insect and eyed the overgrown flower border with disgust. It was her own fault she was in such a fix. If she'd had the foresight to hire someone to take care of the lawn while her mother was in the hospital, she wouldn't have to do this.

For a moment, her thoughts strayed wistfully to her climate-controlled real-estate office in Jacksonville where the plants were made of silk and the only thing that buzzed was the overworked telephone. Two weeks and already she missed that sacred temple of capitalism and free enterprise where she could wheel and deal to her heart's content. Where she could plan power lunches, give full rein to her Type A personality and never waste a passing thought on aphids.

Then she remembered that she'd chosen to leave all that behind. At least temporarily. For the next few weeks she'd be working out of the Morgan's Point office and overseeing her mother's recuperation. Rachel sat on her heels and used the back of her hand to brush her dark hair away from her forehead. She'd just keep reminding herself that she'd volunteered for this.

Gardening in August was grueling work anywhere, but it was double torture in the dense humidity of a Florida afternoon. As a child, Rachel had disliked getting hot and dirty. At twenty-nine, she abhorred it.

She was not the outdoor type and had never known a single moment of gardening joy. She found no comfort in spading up soft earth, in watching seedlings grow strong in the sun or in communing with earthworms. In spite of the big straw hat and sturdy gloves she wore, this unwanted exercise would not do her carefully guarded skin or her French manicure one bit of good.

But if it made her mother happy, she'd manage somehow. She locked the fingers of both hands together and flexed them purposefully before grabbing a clump of suspicious-looking greenery.

"No, Rachel, that's a petunia," Lydia Fox cried in alarm. She pointed with the tip of her cane. "That fuzzy thing next to it is a weed."

"But that one has a flower," Rachel protested.

"I know," Lydia said with a sigh. "But it's still a weed."

"Maybe it's a wildflower." Rachel doubtfully examined the plant in question. "Who am I to deprive a poor little wildflower of life, liberty and the pursuit of pollination?"

"I've never known you to be particularly interested in the protection of wildlife." Lydia smiled at her arch reference to Rachel's battles with Joseph Morgan, the environmentally minded mayor of Morgan's Point.

"Right." Rachel disliked being reminded of her failures; she was not a good sport when it came to losing. And that's exactly what she'd done in her last encounter with the esteemed mayor. The commission she'd lost didn't bother her half as much as knowing she had been bested by an opponent in the business arena.

Thinking about Joe Morgan added a certain ferocity to Rachel's efforts and she yanked the weed out of the ground with the same pleasure she'd get from someday yanking the rug out from under the good-looking attorney.

"There's another one," Lydia pointed out.

Rachel stared doutbfully at the plants. They all looked alike to her. "Are you sure it's a weed?"

"Trust me, dear. Now pull it out before it goes to seed and makes a lot of little weeds."

"You mean it's a mother?"

"Rachel!"

"Okay, okay." She complied, but made it clear that she would rather talk than work. "Aren't weeds really just plants that nobody likes? I mean, if gardeners all over the world suddenly declared petunias persona non grata, wouldn't they show up on the very next 'most unwanted' list?"

Lydia shook her head. "I can see this is not going to work. Maybe I can hire Elizabeth to come over and weed for me."

Rachel brightened. "That's a wonderful idea. I'm sure she'd love the chance to earn some extra money this summer." Ten-year-old Elizabeth Wilton lived down the street. The child had fed and watered Lydia's pet duck during her hospitalization, and was very conscientious. More important, she evidenced no apparent distaste for dirt. Such qualifications made her a wonderful surrogate gardener.

"I wish I could do it myself." The older woman sat on a small garden seat, her injured legs stretched out before her. "I hate being so helpless."

Rachel winced when she heard that shaky, discouraged note creep into her mother's voice. "You are not helpless, Mom. You've come a long way. It's just been three months since the accident and you've only been out of the rehabilitation center for two weeks. Give yourself time. You're going to be fine."

Once her mother's sudden tears were under control, Rachel spread the fuzzy weed on the ground to use as a model for future extractions. Leaning forward on her knees, she braced herself with one hand and stretched to pluck another offender.

She squealed when something latched onto a chunk of her upended derriere and twisted. In her efforts to get away from her attacker, Rachel sprawled facedown in the dirt. She kicked and swatted at her behind. "Damn that duck!"

Lydia pounded the ground with her cane. "Bad girl! Mrs. Puddleduck, let go of Rachel and come here at once!"

Lydia's spoiled pet, a big white duck with jaws of steel, reluctantly released the tender morsel and waddled over to her mistress, quacking indignantly. As if she were the injured party!

Lydia reached down and stroked the ruffled feathers. "You bad, bad girl. You must stop pinching Rachel, do you hear?"

Rachel rubbed her backside gingerly. "I've just about had it with that flesh-eating bird of prey, Mom."

"Oh, Rachel, she's just playing. She'd never really try to hurt you."

"You could have fooled me." Rachel's eyes narrowed on the duck. That was how poultry looked when they gloated. "Be warned, Puddleduck. Bite me one more time and you'll end up on the table next Sunday drenched in orange sauce."

Lydia was appalled by her daughter's ultimatum. She'd received the fluffy yellow duckling as a gift from an admirer and had immediately become attached to the tiny creature.

As far as Rachel was concerned, the duck was no longer cute or fluffy and it had just about worn out its welcome.

"Don't even think such a thing." Lydia's eyes teared up again. "Mrs. Puddleduck means so much to me. I don't know what I'd do without her."

Rachel's behind smarted as she rubbed the bruised flesh through her cotton shorts. "I can make a few suggestions."

The bird stared at Rachel with flat, beady eyes, extended its long neck and began quacking and flapping its wings with a vengeance.

"Oh, shut up!" Rachel demanded. The squawking continued at a higher decibel level. "Mother, do something."

"Hush," Lydia cooed as she scooped her pet onto her lap. The duck quieted immediately and rested her head on Lydia's bosom. "See, Rachel. She's really quite gentle."

"She's a wereduck, is what she is, and she'd better keep her cotton-picking bill away from my behind. I won't tolerate being trifled with."

"Good afternoon, ladies," Joe Morgan greeted as he stepped around the side of the house. He'd arrived just in time to hear Rachel's remarks and considered the last one fair warning. Not only for the duck, but for himself, as well. Way back in his young and foolish days, he'd once fancied himself in love with another pushy, career-minded female. He'd barely escaped with his manhood and his pride intact.

He had nothing against women in general; in fact he loved them. He wasn't one of those bitter types who, once burned, was willing to freeze for fear of the fire. No, sir. At thirty-three, he was ready to take his family's advice and settle down. He was, in fact, actively looking for a woman with whom to share his life.

He knew exactly what he wanted: a soft, pliable, womanly woman. One he could love and protect and who would love and nurture him in return. One who didn't feel a feminist compulsion to compete with him on every level and who could find fulfillment and satisfaction in him, his career, his children. One who was willing to stand beside her man, or maybe even a bit behind him if the occasion called. Perhaps such notions were considered archaic in some circles, but a small-town politician's wife had to be a special breed.

What he didn't want, and certainly didn't need, was a woman as tough and opinionated as Rachel Fox. She was so calm and ruthless, it was downright scary. The sheer force of her personality wouldn't allow her to stand by her man; she'd always want to be way out in front. Dragging him in her wake by the ring in his nose.

So what if she was a knockout? So what if her dark, silky hair, cat-shaped hazel eyes, and flawless ivory skin gave her an almost exotic beauty? Like the old folks said, beauty was only skin-deep. Scratch that porcelain-perfect surface and you'd find flint and steel underneath. Maybe she was attractive, but only a fool would place his mental health in jeopardy by violating Rachel Fox's personal space.

At the first sound of the deep bass voice, Rachel scrambled to her feet and stripped off her gloves. A nice, squishy earthworm pressed firmly into Morgan's outstretched hand would wipe that self-assured politician's grin off his face. But since there were never any invertebrates around when you needed one, she took his hand and gave it a half-hearted shake.

She knew she had dirt streaks on her face, but she made no attempt to wipe them off. She wouldn't give him the satisfaction of knowing that he had rattled her with his unexpected appearance.

Actually, it was more his appearance than the unexpected nature of his visit that had done most of the rattling. Just because the two of them held diametrically opposed opinions on every issue under the sun, didn't mean that she couldn't appreciate favorable genetics and testosterone at its best.

Joe Morgan was just over six feet tall and well built. He wore pleated tan slacks and a light blue shirt with the cuffs turned back on strong, hairy forearms. His tie was loosened at his neck and he carried a scuffed leather briefcase. Rachel contended that one could tell a lot about a man by his shoes. Morgan's were comfortable, expensive loafers. Nicely polished.

He wore his dark brown hair fashionably short, which drew attention to the masculine proportions of his features: strong jaw, good cheekbones, nice nose. His eyes were light brown, so friendly that they made you forget not to trust him. His shoulders were just wide enough, his waist just slim enough, to suggest strength without bulk. His skin was tanned to a shade of Florida bronze that said he'd never heard of skin cancer or the damaging effects of UV rays.

Worst of all, he had a wide, honest smile that belied his devious nature and a down-home charm that he used skillfully on those willing to be charmed. She wasn't.

The boy-next-door good looks of Kevin Costner, coupled with the earnest integrity of a young Jimmy Stewart made it easy to see why the mayor was such a popular man about town. Even if the town was Morgan's Point, whose population of three thousand probably included a number of gators and raccoons. As she looked him over appraisingly, the phrase "big fish in a little pond" came to mind.

"Well, well, well, the Honorable Mayor Morgan in person," Rachel said with enough sarcasm to cover her uncomfortable awareness of him. "If you're out politicking for reelection, you're wasting your time. I'm not registered to vote in this district."

"I am," Lydia piped up. "It's not election time already, is it, Joe?"

"I still have a year of my current term left."

"So is this visit prompted by business or pleasure?" Rachel asked with a nod at the slim briefcase.

"It's always a pleasure to call on the lovely Fox ladies," he said. "However, this is a professional call."

"Well, get on with it," Rachel snapped. "I have work to do."

"Rachel!" Lydia sent her a quelling glance. "You'll have to forgive my daughter's lack of manners, Joe. She's been in the city too long. Pay her no notice."

"It's hard not to notice the prettiest woman in town, Mrs. Fox. Present company excluded, of course."

Lydia blushed like a schoolgirl and Rachel rolled her eyes. Maybe her mother was taken in by such bald-faced flattery, but she didn't buy it for a minute.

They moved to the shade of the terrace and Lydia sat down on a white wrought-iron chaise longue. Joe leaned over and spoke to her in a confidential tone. "Rachel's still miffed because I came out on top in our last little skirmish." When he turned to Rachel, the warmth in his brown eyes cooled. "You strike me as the type of woman who always wants to be on top."

Rachel bristled, but refused to be sidetracked by sexual innuendo. "Your interference cost me a lot of money, Morgan. I'd hardly use a word as benign as *miffed* to describe my feelings for you."

"And I'd hate to discuss anything more intense in front of your mother. Maybe we should get together sometime and sort it all out." Joe regretted his words as soon as he spoke them. No way did he want to get involved with another hard-nosed, ambitious woman whose only desires were success and power. There'd been a lesson in that fiasco, and no one could say Joe Morgan wasn't a fast learner.

But seeing Rachel in her present state, with smudges on her face, her dark hair wind-mussed and little beads of moisture on her upper lip, he could almost forget how calculating she could be. She looked like any other devoted daughter, doing something she obviously disliked to please a mother she loved. Maybe she did care about something besides money.

Standing so close that he could see the gentle pulse at the base of her throat, he was unable to resist the impulse to touch her. "You have dirt on your face."

"What?" she demanded.

"Here," he said as he reached out and brushed her cheek. "And here." He drew a line across her jaw. As much as he wanted to deny it, there was something inherently appealing about Rachel Fox. He'd recognized it the first time he'd seen her.

She'd been all business that day in January when she'd bustled into his office. She'd come with a bulging portfolio and an offer from a Jacksonville developer to purchase the property outside of town known as Cypress Knoll.

Ordinarily, he wouldn't have wasted any time showing a hotshot real-estate broker the door. But he'd listened to Rachel. Not just because she was beautiful, which she was. But because she was so sure of herself and because she didn't use the fact that she was beautiful to her advantage.

She must have been aware of his attraction to her; at the time he hadn't tried to hide it. Nevertheless, she maintained her professional demeanor, never acknowledging that attraction or giving any indication that she might be attracted in return. Her lack of interest had presented an intriguing challenge at the time. It still did.

When she'd finished her sales talk, he'd rejected her offer. Refusing to take "no" for an answer, she'd invited him to dinner to continue her pitch. Thanking her for the invitation, he assured her that it would be a waste of their time unless she was willing to consider a different kind of relationship.

Her poise had slipped a bit then and she'd called him a few unflattering names, accusing him of unethical behavior bordering on sexual harrassment.

He'd explained that since they weren't doing business, he hadn't overstepped any professional boundaries. After giving him the verbal equivalent of a slap in the face, she'd stormed out, taking her offer to the town council. She'd put up a good fight, but in the end, he'd won. Partly because he was a sixth-generation Morgan whose ancestors had founded the town and she was an outsider. But mostly because he was right and she was wrong.

Pushing back her wide-brimmed hat, Rachel stepped out of his reach, obeying an internal warning that had sounded the instant he touched her. It had been over six months since his stubbornness had ruined her deal with MegaMont Development, but that caress was a powerful reminder of the unwanted attraction she'd felt at the time. He'd cost her thousands of dollars in commissions, so what did she care how long his eyelashes were?

She hid her discomfort in bluster. "Surely, you didn't come here to point out my grooming deficiencies, Mayor."

Joe appreciated Rachel's snappy retorts even if they did reflect a one-track mind. All she ever thought about was business. "I wanted to stop by and welcome you to Morgan's Point. I'm sorry it took me so long, but I've been too busy to get by before."

"I can understand a lawyer being swamped in this town," she said dryly. "The place is a veritable hotbed of criminal activity."

Joe grinned. Everyone in town knew his practice was more civil than criminal, and so did Rachel. Cagey customers like her made it their business to know everything about their opponents. Even their weaknesses. "I've been working with the committee planning the Autumn Festival."

"Ah, yes. The highlight of Morgan's Point's social season. Have you chosen Miss Cypress Stump yet?"

"That's Miss Cypress Knoll. And as a matter of fact, we haven't. Do you want to throw your hat into the ring?"

Rachel wanted to throw Joe Morgan into Lake Sampson. "I'm pretty busy myself these days."

"It's just as well. Candidates for the title are considerably younger."

Rachel winced at the reference to her age. With thirty looming on the horizon, it had become a sensitive subject. "I guess you didn't get to be mayor without learning how to push people's buttons."

"What can I say? We all have our talents."

"And our shortcomings," she said with false cheerfulness.

"Rachel, where are your manners, dear?" Lydia asked from her shady spot on the chaise longue.

"I've found that manners don't get you far in the world." She directed her next words at Joe. "But determination does."

"Feel free to demonstrate your determination however you want," he said affably. "Just don't go drumming up business for yourself at the expense of Morgan's Point."

As bantering as their conversation had been, Rachel was well aware of his professional opposition. He had drawn the battle lines and obviously expected her to back off. He didn't know her very well.

"You seem confused, Mayor, about what may or may not be good for this town. If my proposal had been approved, it would have brought in jobs and tourist revenue. It would have jump-started an economy whose biggest attraction is currently amateur day at Cooter Bob's School of Gator Wrestling."

Joe laughed in spite of her exaggerated slur on his hometown. "I guess you haven't heard. Cooter Bob had to close up shop. The place was costing him an arm and a leg."

His unexpected remark made Rachel laugh despite her determination not to be charmed. So, he had a sense of humor. Just so he didn't misconstrue her momentary lapse as bonding.

"Cooter Bob's?" Lydia asked. "I never heard of the place."

Lydia's injuries made it difficult for her to recognize a joke, so Rachel explained it. By the time she was finished, the temporary truce was over.

"I plan to pursue my efforts to enlighten the people of this town," Rachel told Joe. "Your unwillingness to compromise has held them back long enough."

Joe stiffened. No one had the best interests of Morgan's Point more firmly in mind than he, and he resented Rachel's unfair accusations. "At the rate you're going, you'll probably need the services of a good attorney. When you do, let me know. I'll give you a discount."

Rachel fumed inwardly, but her smile was saccharine. "Oh, I'll call you all right, Mayor Morgan. When hell freezes over and pigs fly."

Chapter Two

"Rachel Estelle Fox! What is wrong with you?" Lydia was confused by the pair's verbal sparring. "Joe doesn't know you like I do. He might not understand that you're just teasing."

"No, Mrs. Fox," Joe assured her. "Rachel and I understand each other fine. Don't we, Rachel?"

"We sure do. Now will you kindly state your business and go find some other hapless citizens to annoy?"

"Rachel!" Lydia's dismay was increasing.

"Don't concern yourself, Mrs. Fox," Joe said. "I only came by to tell you that we had a town council meeting last night."

Lydia smiled. "Did you? I've lost track of time since the accident." She turned to her daughter. "What did you make for lunch, dear? We'll invite Joe to join us."

"We had lunch two hours ago, Mom."

Lydia looked puzzled. "Are you sure?"

"Yes, Mom." Life had changed for the Fox women one morning last May. Lydia had been taking a contract to the closing company when she was struck by a car attempting a right turn. Fortunately the driver was going slow enough to stop immediately, but the impact had left her mother with two fractured legs and a slight head injury that required two months of acute rehabilitation.

The physical therapists had assured them that with continued effort, Lydia would regain full unassisted mobility. The cane was a temporary precaution to aid balance. Rachel saw to it that her mother was faithful in doing her prescribed exercises and careful not to overuse the newly mended limbs.

The prognosis was not so good, however, for Lydia's recovery from the emotional changes and mild cognitive deficits resulting from the head injury. These worried Rachel more than any residual physical problems Lydia might have.

She took her mother's memory lapses in stride, but a frown creased Joe's high, smooth forehead. Her eyes met his for a moment and she saw something she didn't like. Concern. Damn, Morgan wasn't supposed to have tender feelings.

Her gaze jerked back to her mother, grateful for an excuse to leave his company. "If you're hungry, Mom, I'll make you a snack."

"Oh, no, I never eat between meals. I am between meals now, aren't I?"

"Yes, Mom."

Lydia brightened. "Maybe Joe would like something. Do you eat between meals, Joe?"

"Yes, ma'am, I do."

"Wonderful! Rachel made a lemon chess pie this morning. Would you like a piece?"

He looked at Rachel and raised a brow. "I do have a weakness for tart things, but I don't have time today."

Rachel recognized the innuendo that went right over her mother's head. "Too bad. One piece of my pie and you'd be cured of that weakness."

"I don't doubt it for a minute." Joe ran a hand through his hair. The woman had a knack for making him forget she wasn't his type. "As I was saying, something came up at the meeting last night."

Rachel braced for a fight. "Unless the town has decided to sell that property to my client, we have nothing to discuss."

"This has nothing to do with you. It concerns your mother and ah...Mrs. Puddleduck. Bertie Caldwell filed a complaint."

Lydia frowned. "A complaint about what?"

"Your duck."

"My duck?" Lydia clapped her hand over her mouth. "Has this bad girl bitten Bertie Caldwell's posterior, too?"

Joe grinned. "Not as far as I know."

Lydia waved her hand dismissively. "Bertie's just jealous because Ernie Baxter is sweet on me instead of her. He's the one who gave me Mrs. Puddleduck."

"Mrs. Caldwell didn't mention Ernie," Joe said. "She just wants Mrs. Puddleduck to stay away from downtown."

Lydia looked confused. "I don't understand."

"I'm afraid you'll have to leave her home from now on. No more leading her around on a silk ribbon like a modern-day Mother Goose." In truth, the children loved to watch Lydia and her plump duck strolling down Main Street. Why, he knew adults who kept dried corn kernels in their pockets so they could give the preening bird a treat when she waddled by.

Most people liked the unorthodox duo and were well aware of how the duckling's clandestine visit to the intensive-care unit helped rouse Lydia from a coma after her accident. There'd even been a story about it in the *Weekly Guardian.*

Rachel wasn't overly fond of the bird, but Bertie Caldwell's ambush was spiteful and mean-spirited. "Who died and left that old busybody in charge of the streets of Morgan's Point?"

"Mrs. Caldwell isn't in charge," Joe replied. "It's the law."

"The law?" Rachel asked skeptically.

"Actually, it's a city ordinance. As mayor, it's my duty to see that it's enforced."

"Law enforcement sounds like a job for the police," Rachel pointed out.

"It is, normally," Joe agreed. "But since I'm a friend of the family, I offered to come over and talk to Lydia." The truth was, no one on the town council or the police force had wanted the unpleasant task of exiling Mrs. Puddleduck. Not even the overzealous Officer Hacker who'd been known to issue citations for spitting on the sidewalk.

Rachel snorted. Friend of the family, indeed! Joe Morgan was no friend of hers. Before she could comment on that, Lydia spoke up.

"Except for occasionally pinching Rachel's tushy, Mrs. Puddleduck hasn't caused any trouble." Her eyes filled with sudden tears as she stroked the duck. Emotional weakness was another side effect of the accident.

Joe felt like the villain in a melodrama. Next thing you knew, he'd be evicting widows and orphans. "I know.

But there's been a complaint, so I'd like you to keep her penned from now on."

"Mrs. Puddleduck hates the pen, but I guess I could try."

"Oh, brother." Rachel resented her mother's obvious willingness to accomodate Morgan. Feeling an overwhelming need to get away from Joe, she went back to picking weeds.

"That's a petunia, dear," Lydia called out before putting her hand on Joe's arm. "Ernie asked me to marry him, you know."

Topic maintenance was not one of her mother's strong suits. Rachel stopped torturing the greenery and returned to the patio. "Mom. You never told me Ernie asked you to marry him."

"I guess I forgot." Lydia sighed. "My memory isn't what it used to be. Let me think. I was still at the rehab center, in a wheelchair. The doctors weren't sure if I would walk again."

"Now that you're recovering so nicely," Joe said, "are you going to take Ernie up on his offer?"

Lydia shrugged. "I haven't decided. I don't feel like the same person I was before the accident. It wasn't until I nearly died that I realized I hadn't been living. I have a lot of lost time to make up for.

"I married when I was nineteen," she went on. "Went right from my father's house to my husband's. I never worked at a paying job or learned how to take care of myself. I had Molly, my oldest daughter, a couple of years later."

"I've never met her," Joe commented.

"Molly's a doctor. She's running a clinic on a reservation up in Montana to pay her medical school debts. She'll be coming home for good soon."

"She didn't come when you had your accident?" he asked.

"I wouldn't let Rachel tell her how serious it was," she said conspiratorially. "I didn't want her to worry. Her patients needed her more than I did—she's the only doctor for miles around."

Lydia seemed lost in thought. Several moments passed before she spoke again. "I had a son but I lost him at birth. For years, all I did was keep house and take care of my family." She pointed a finger at Joe. "Not that those aren't important jobs."

"Most young women today feel differently, but I agree. A woman's place is in the home."

"Wait just a darn minute," Rachel interjected.

"Don't interrupt, dear, I'm talking to Joe," Lydia reproved. "When Harvey died I didn't know what to do. Rachel had to make the arrangements. It was a difficult time."

"I'm sure it was," Joe agreed. He didn't know why Mrs. Fox was telling him all this, but the least he could do was listen.

"Mom," Rachel said gently, "Mayor Morgan is a busy man. He probably needs to leave now." Her mother's outpouring made Rachel uncomfortable; she never revealed herself in such a manner. She played life close to the vest.

"Do you need to go, Joe?" Lydia asked.

He checked his watch, then smiled perversely at Rachel. "Not just yet."

Lydia lost her train of thought and started telling him about her garden. When it became obvious that no more family secrets would be spilled, Rachel stopped listening and went back to weeding.

Her mother's remarks brought painful memories. When her dad had died, they'd been faced with serious financial problems. He'd depleted the family savings and borrowed on his life insurance to pay the girls' college expenses. In the midst of their grief, they'd had to re-group.

A naive twenty-year-old, Rachel dropped out of college and went to real-estate school in hopes of making some fast money. Molly, a first-year medical student, borrowed heavily from the government's physician loan program, agreeing to repay the debt by later working where she was needed.

It took Lydia years to fully recover from the shock of her husband's death. Finally, Rachel convinced her to attend real-estate school and when she was ready, she eased the older woman into the job market.

Having seen what happened to women who were emotionally and financially dependent on a man, Rachel knew she would always take care of herself. She worked hard, earned her broker's license and started her own business, eventually opening the branch in Morgan's Point for Lydia. In nine years, she had climbed to the top of a competitive field. Business acumen and determination had gotten her there, but it was fear of dependence that made her stay.

When the conversation lagged, Rachel turned to her mother. "You look a little pale. Do you want to go in-side?"

"No, but I'd like some lemonade. How about you, Joe?"

"I told you I like tart things."

"I'll get it." Rachel stood and dusted the seat of her shorts. She was quickly reminded of Mrs. Puddleduck's attack. Giving the bird a dirty look on her way to the house, she muttered another warning. "I have an excellent recipe for Peking duck."

Mrs. Puddleduck squawked an indignant reply.

Without invitation, Joe followed her inside.

She washed her hands and removed three glasses and a tray from the cupboard before acknowledging his presence.

"I suppose this means you're staying," she said without looking at him.

Normally, Joe didn't like using caveman tactics, but Rachel wasn't a woman who appreciated subtlety. He gently grasped her arms and turned her to face him.

"Get your hands off me. What do you think you're doing?" she demanded.

"I want to conduct a little experiment."

"What kind of experiment?"

"Chemistry," he said as his lips covered hers.

He felt her resist, but he didn't let go. He couldn't have stopped, even if he'd wanted to. Then he heard a soft murmur of surrender as her lips parted to give him sweet access.

The warmth of Joe's touch was pervasive and seemed to melt Rachel's bones. At least her knees felt too wobbly to hold her upright and she was forced to hold on to him for support. She experienced the quiet insistence of his kiss in several areas of her body simultaneously; her pulse quickened, her mind fogged over and some undefinable part of her hungered for more.

Gradually she became aware of the tangy scent of his after-shave, of the starched coolness of his shirt, of the rough prickle of his five o'clock shadow.

As the assault on her senses continued, she was dismayed to discover that Joe excited her as no man ever had. It frightened her that he wielded such power over her. Power meant control and she had never let any man control her. She wouldn't start with Joe Morgan. When he moaned deep in his throat, she twisted out of his arms and took two steps backward.

Breathing hard, she tried to regain her lost composure. When she finally spoke, her tone was much cooler than she felt. "I thought I'd already given you explicit instructions on where you could stuff your personal propositions."

"Hell, Rachel," he said with a grin. "You know that's anatomically impossible."

"All I know is that I don't care to have any more dealings with you, professional or personal. So get out."

Joe ran his hand through his hair in frustration. The gesture would probably become a habit if he spent much more time with Rachel. "Believe it or not, I feel the same."

"Then why did you kiss me like that?" she demanded. "Of all the Cro-Magnon things to do..."

He shook his head, as confused as she was. "Damned if I know. It's just something I've wanted to do since I first saw you. My mind is well aware that you're not the kind of woman I want, but my body won't pay attention."

"Which only reinforces my opinion that the brain is not the most highly developed male organ. Do the words *chauvinist pig* ring a bell, Morgan?"

He grinned because he knew it would only make her madder. "Is that one of those little pot-bellied pigs people keep as pets nowadays?"

"Get out!" she reiterated in a voice that strived for control.

"After you lost the council's support last January, you slammed into my office and told me where to go. You didn't give me a chance to defend myself before you slammed right out again.''

"I made a decision that wasn't open for discussion.'' She took the lemonade from the refrigerator and kicked the door shut with her foot.

"I was actually relieved when you went running back to Jacksonville and refused to take my calls. Being ignored by you was like being yanked back from the edge of a cliff—I didn't want to fall, but I had a self-destructive fascination to experience it.''

Rachel didn't know what to make of his confession. "Give me a break.''

"If it hadn't been for your mother's accident, you probably wouldn't have come back to Morgan's Point at all and we wouldn't be having this conversation.''

"News flash, Morgan. We *aren't* having this conversation.'' She sloshed lemonade into the glasses and picked up the tray. "And for your information, I would have come back anyway. As soon as I had an offer for Cypress Knoll that your precious town council couldn't refuse.''

"Is business the only thing you ever think about?'' Joe wished now that he'd shown more restraint where his impulses and his big mouth were concerned. It had been stupid to kiss her; stupider yet to reveal his feelings. Still, for a moment there, he'd felt her eager response.

"What else is there?''

"Don't you have a private life?''

She glanced over her shoulder as she went out the patio door. "Not with you, I don't.''

Joe closed the door with a thud and followed her. "I don't like this chemistry thing any more than you do, but I don't see how we can get it out of our systems if you refuse to talk to me.''

"I don't need to get you out of my system. You were never in." She had no intention of ever acknowledging the unwanted attraction she felt. She disliked everything Joe Morgan stood for. She glanced around the yard and watched as her mother turned away from the flower border and limped toward the patio.

Joe scowled. For his own well-being, he should run fast and far from this woman, but he couldn't bring himself to take the first step. "What exactly is it about me that you don't like? Tell me. I can take it. Do I smell bad or have dirty habits?"

"You smell quite nice. But I don't want to know you well enough to discover your habits." Rachel set the tray down and took a big gulp of lemonade.

"You're a coward, Rachel," Joe said between clenched teeth. "You're afraid of what could happen between us. I know you're attracted to me as much as I am to you."

"You're crazy."

"Why are you fighting it? I think we should go ahead and find out where this could lead. Get it over with, as it were."

"You are the most egotistical, pompous, conceited..."

When words failed her, Joe supplied, "Chauvinist pig?"

"That's right." She walked to the edge of the patio and took her mother's arm. Lydia's presence would put an end to this ridiculous conversation. Mrs. Puddleduck took offense at Rachel's intrusion and nipped her on the ankle.

"Ouch! You stupid duck."

"She's very protective of me." Lydia excused the animal's behavior to Joe.

He chuckled as he helped the older woman into a chair. "Just don't bring her downtown again."

"Mother can take that duck anywhere she wants," Rachel said as she rubbed her ankle. "It's a free country."

"Why are you being so hardheaded?" Joe asked. "You don't even like the damn duck. I heard you threaten her with orange sauce."

"My feelings for the damn duck are irrelevant. The point is, you have no right to come here and tell us what to do."

"Children, children, don't fuss," Lydia reprimanded.

"You can't tell us where we can or cannot take our duck." Rachel was determined to have the last word.

"*Our* duck?" he asked.

"Her duck."

"I came here as a friend. Mrs. Caldwell did some research and found a city ordinance that makes it illegal to keep livestock within the city limits."

"A duck is not livestock," Rachel protested.

"It's poultry. And poultry is considered livestock." He reached into the briefcase he'd set beside his chair and pulled out a photocopy of the original ordinance and passed it to Rachel.

She looked it over. "This is a hundred years old. It was meant to keep people from raising goats in the middle of town."

"Livestock, Rachel. Any livestock. The law is clear."

"It's an outdated and obsolete law," she fired back. "It should be changed."

"Children!" Lydia scolded. "Please be civil."

Joe turned to the older woman. "Mrs. Caldwell wanted me to force you to get rid of Mrs. Puddleduck completely, but I managed to talk her into being satisfied that you wouldn't bring her to town. Can I assure her that you're agreeable to that?"

Rachel could tell by the look on Lydia's face that her mother was about to bow down to the almighty authority—*man*. "If my mother wants to take her duck downtown, she will."

Lydia frowned, clearly confused about her part in this, as her gaze traveled from Rachel to Joe, then back again.

Joe looked sternly at Rachel. "I have no doubt that you will do as you please, but it would be wise for you to think about the repercussions if you go against the law."

Rachel planted her feet and put her hands on her hips. "And if I do, will you have me arrested?"

Joe wasn't sure to what lengths she was willing to go and somehow he knew better than to issue an ultimatum. "That would be within my power."

"I'm frightened." Rachel's nonchalance belied her words. "You may have political power in this town, Morgan. But I have an unlimited supply of willpower."

Joe slowly counted to ten before he replied. He would have called it stubborn obstinance, but why split hairs? It could only make her actions more rash. "Oh, lady. I'm well aware of that."

Chapter Three

After Joe left in a huff, Mrs. Puddleduck maintained a low profile and Rachel finished weeding one section of the flower bed in record time. She simply imagined that each fuzzy green invader was Joe Morgan's head and the chore became almost a pleasure.

Later, when red-haired Elizabeth dropped by, Rachel negotiated a deal with the child to finish the job at her convenience. The little girl seemed pleased to have the opportunity to play in the dirt and get paid for it at the same time.

After the evening meal, Lydia leaned against the counter so she could dry dishes while Rachel washed. "What is it about Joe Morgan that upsets you so, my dear?"

Rachel scrubbed a dirty plate furiously. For someone so absentminded, her mother didn't miss much. "He's stubborn and uncompromising. He can't see anyone's viewpoint but his own. He's already ruined one big deal for me and if he has his way, I'll never get the council to sell Cypress Knoll."

"Stubborn and uncompromising?" Lydia smiled as she repeated thoughtfully. "Hmm, maybe you two have more in common than I thought."

"Mother!"

"It's too bad. There was a time when I thought you two might become a couple."

"In your dreams, Mom." Rachel put the dishes away and was none-too-gentle handling her mother's china. "I'll never see eye to eye with Mr. Macho."

"Never say never." Lydia put the glasses away herself. "I wish you would find a good man, settle down and give me some grandkids."

"I'm only twenty-nine."

"*Only* twenty-nine?"

Rachel ignored yet another crack about her age. "I don't need a man to settle down."

Lydia eyed her reproachfully. "You don't mean you'd have one of those artificial babies, do you?"

"Of course not. All I meant was that I own my own business and my own home. I have a brand-new BMW and just about anything else a woman could want. What do I need a man for?"

Lydia raised a skeptical brow. "Really, dear. I thought we had that talk when you were thirteen."

"You know what I mean. I'm not about to pin all my hopes on a man, only to have them crash down around me when he leaves."

"Your father didn't abandon us, Rachel. He didn't plan to die so young," her mother said softly.

"I know. But you have to admit that if you hadn't depended on him so much, you wouldn't have been so desperate when he died and Molly wouldn't be in Montana."

"And you wouldn't have had to quit college."

"I don't regret that," Rachel insisted. "I've done all right. We don't have to worry about money anymore. Business is good, our investments are paying off. We're finally secure."

"I guess Harvey thought there'd be plenty of time to save for our old age," her mother said as a single tear rolled down her cheek. "He'd never been sick a day in his life and there was no way of knowing his heart was bad. Even with the way things turned out, I have no regrets about the way we lived. Your father made me very happy."

"I don't want to depend on a man to make me happy, Mom. I believe in making myself happy."

"If you're hard, it's my fault for letting you take the brunt of everything after your father died."

Rachel hugged her mother and kissed her cheek. Then she smiled. "I'm not hard, Mom. I'm tough. There's a difference."

"Sometimes I think you're too tough. You keep yourself all bottled up. It worries me."

They finished the dishes and Rachel was relieved to also finish that topic of conversation. She handed Lydia her cane. "You should go freshen up. Ernie will probably come to call."

"Probably," Lydia agreed unenthusiastically.

"Why the frown? I thought you enjoyed spending time with him."

"I used to," Lydia corrected. "He used to be so exciting, but since the accident, he's been..."

"Mom, has Ernie done anything...well...you know?" Rachel was at a loss for words. These were the kind of questions her mother had asked her as a teenager. When had their roles reversed?

"No, that's the problem. He used to be hot to trot, if you know what I mean. He's changed since the accident."

Rachel was inclined to think it was her mother who had changed. The old Lydia would never have used terms like "hot to trot."

Lydia lowered her voice and whispered confidentially, "I've been dropping hints, but he's just an old stick-in-the-mud. Maybe he's too old for me."

Rachel groaned. In the past, her mother would not have voiced such an opinion, even if she'd had one. "Mom, you're still recovering. Only an unfeeling brute would hit on you now."

"I'm not dead, Rachel. I'm a lot older than you, but I still long for the same things. I want romance. I want to feel a man's touch. I want Ernie to hold more than just my hand. The only time he even does that much is to help me in and out of my chair. Like I'm some old lady!"

Rachel was uncomfortable having this conversation with her mother. She phrased her next question carefully. "Were you and Ernie...very close...before?"

"Not quite." Lydia giggled. "He used to spend hours trying to seduce me, but I was holding out for marriage."

"I'm confused. If you were holding out for marriage before, why haven't you accepted his proposal?"

"There's plenty of fish in the sea." Lydia patted her daughter's shoulder. "I'm willing to bait my hook and see what happens. Not like some people who don't even realize it when they've snagged a big one."

"I don't know what you mean, Mom."

"Don't play innocent, dear. I may be a little impulsive and forgetful at times, but I'm not deaf. I heard all those little innuendoes Joe Morgan flung your way today. And

I saw the way your eyes lit up every time you glanced in his direction."

"My eyes lit up because the man infuriates me with his mere presence," Rachel protested.

"Whatever you say, dear. Just remember, you can fool yourself, but you can't fool your mother. If you'll excuse me, I need to change into something sexy for Ernie. I'm going to try to drive him crazy." She made her way slowly down the hall.

Rachel was still staring after her, trying to figure out what her mother had been talking about, when someone knocked on the back door. She opened it, expecting to see Ernie Baxter's steel-gray crew cut and was surprised to find her old friend, Clay Cusak, standing on the patio. His family had lived next to hers for years in Jacksonville and they'd grown up together.

"Still coming to the back door, Clay?" She greeted him with a brotherly kiss. "Sorry, we're all out of cookies."

"Hi, beautiful. I just happened to be in the neighborhood and thought—"

She laughed. "You'd come by and mooch some dinner."

He glanced over her shoulder at the sparkling kitchen. "Ah, shucks, I'm too late. Well, never mind that. I've come to take you away from all of this."

She put her hands on her hips. "The last time I accepted an offer from you, I ended up at a female mudwrestling competition."

"You have a good memory, Rach," he remarked as he walked past her into the living room. "I still say you should have challenged the champ. You could have whipped her, hands down."

"I'll never forgive you for that, Clay." Rachel laughed at the memory of that long-ago night. "I thought we'd have to fight our way out of the place. And me dressed in a raw silk suit and heels."

He chuckled. "The look on your face was priceless when that big galoot ripped off his T-shirt and offered to lend it to you."

Lydia came into the room. "Why, Clay, when did you get here? Have you had your supper?"

"I had something at the drugstore," he said, hugging Lydia and smothering her with noisy kisses. "I can't believe I let Ernie Baxter win my favorite woman away from me."

"I thought I was your favorite woman," Rachel said in a mock-injured tone.

"Nope. You're up there, but you're a close second. Lydia, my Lydia, will always be tops."

"Was it really me, Clay, or my homemade cookies?" the older woman asked. "You can tell me the truth after all these years."

"I don't even remember the cookies," he said innocently.

Lydia swatted him playfully. "You ate enough of them to sink a battleship. You're a brash boy and full of blarney, Clay Cusak. But you've more than made up for the son I lost."

"Gosh, Mom, don't get all sentimental on me," he said as he toed the carpet dramatically. Then, without waiting for an invitation, he plopped down on the sofa.

"I like your outfit," he remarked. "New, is it?"

Lydia nodded. "I had to buy all new things. My closet was full of polyester when I got home from the hospital."

Clay looked at Rachel, who shrugged helplessly. "She gave away all her clothes."

"I didn't like that stuff," she explained. "I can't imagine why I'd buy so many little-old-lady dresses."

Clay jumped up and hugged her. "Because you are a little old lady, Mom."

"I'm fifty-five, not a hundred and five. I'm going to be more 'with it' from now on."

"Good for you."

"Don't encourage her," Rachel moaned.

Lydia patted her salt-and-pepper hair worn in a dated, matronly style. "What do you think I should do with this hair?"

"Mom," Rachel said with alarm. "Don't do anything impulsive with your hair."

"A new cut? Or a different color?" Lydia persisted.

"I say go for it, toots. Whatever floats your boat." Clay ducked to avoid the punch Rachel swung in his direction.

"I told you not to encourage her."

"Why don't you fix Clay a sandwich, dear?" Lydia asked.

"He said he ate already."

"He's always hungry. Just go."

Rachel wondered why her mother wanted her out of the room, but she complied, lingering long enough on the other side of the door to eavesdrop shamelessly.

"I do things that worry Rachel," Lydia told Clay when she thought they were alone.

"Like what?"

"Forgetting. I had no memory of buying the clothes in my closet. Don't you think that's strange?"

"Not at all," Clay said matter-of-factly. "You suffered an injury to the brain. Memory lapses are a common result. No big deal."

"Sometimes I start to do something. Then I forget what it is I wanted to do," Lydia said with a frown. "I forget the names of people I've known for years."

Clay covered her hands with his. "The doctors warned you that could happen from time to time."

"I know," she said sadly. "But it upsets Rachel and I'm afraid she'll never believe I'm capable of living on my own. She needs to get on with her own life, not sit around here worrying about me."

"You're the one who needs to stop worrying. Rachel's a big girl—she can take care of herself."

Rachel went into the kitchen to make Clay's sandwich and returned in time to hear her mother remark, "I'm afraid she'll never get married."

"Maybe not. I've proposed to her at least a dozen times and she turns me down flat every time."

"You're a born bachelor, Clay," Rachel said as she handed him his food. "You go through girlfriends like most men go through socks. If I ever took your proposals seriously, you'd fall down with a heart attack."

"Try me," he challenged. "I know several good cardiologists."

"I always wished you were my son." Lydia sighed. "I have two daughters, you know. Maybe you should forget about Rachel and try your luck with Molly. She'll be home in a few months."

"As much as I'd like to be part of this family, I'm afraid I'll have to pass. Molly barely tolerated me as a kid and things didn't get better as we grew up."

Rachel had always thought of Clay as a brother and the two of them were very close. Not so, Clay and Molly.

Rachel's sister, who was four years older, always considered herself too grown-up to have anything to do with grubby children.

Rachel's gaze swept Clay's tall frame from the top of his well-shaped head to the tips of his worn cowboy boots. Boy, was her big sister in for a surprise when she came home. Her little playmate wasn't grubby anymore. In fact, he was positively gorgeous. His flaxen hair had matured into a dark blond, streaked by the sun. The freckles had faded, but the old mischief still sparkled in his eyes, giving him an irresistible charm that lit up a room when he entered. He had an outrageous sense of humor and a reputation for being the life of every party. Clay Cusak was the most essentially happy person Rachel knew.

As attractive as he was, he ignited no spark within her. She knew him and all his secrets too well for there to be any mystery between them. Since childhood, he'd claimed to love her, but Rachel was firm that they could never be more than best buddies. Since she'd come to Morgan's Point, they'd renewed their friendship and he seemed reconciled to the idea.

Clay shivered melodramatically. "Molly's a cold woman. That's why Montana's such a good place for her. She doesn't have to worry about accidentally thawing out up there."

"Whoa, pal." Rachel held up her hand. "That's my sister you're talking about."

Lydia frowned. "You just don't know her well enough, Clay. Why, Molly's the warmest, most caring and compassionate person in the world. That's why she became a doctor."

Clay laughed. "I thought she became a doctor so she could cut people's hearts out and get paid for it."

The doorbell rang as Lydia chastised her "son." Rachel answered it and invited Ernie Baxter inside. The older man stood on the threshhold and greeted each one in turn. Then, smiling shyly for an ex-Marine sergeant, he said formally to Lydia, "I thought we might go for a little ride, my dear. It's a lovely night for gazing at the stars."

When Lydia nodded her consent, Ernie assisted her to her feet and handed her the cane.

As soon as the door closed behind them, Clay turned to Rachel and said suggestively, "Why don't we go out back and do some stargazing of our own? Just you and me and the man in the moon."

"And Mrs. Puddleduck in her pen, quacking to raise the dead." Rachel sank down on the edge of the chair at the opposite end of the room. She'd never taken Clay's propositions seriously before and she wouldn't start now. Even if it was in his nature to push the issue.

Outside, Joe Morgan stepped up on Lydia Fox's front porch. He'd seen the older woman leaving with Ernie Baxter and hoped to speak to Rachel alone. He had a good excuse for returning so soon; he'd forgotten his briefcase this afternoon and he needed it for some work he wanted to catch up on at the office.

He was about to ring the bell when he heard the deep ring of male laughter through the screen door and realized that Rachel was not alone after all. When he heard the carefree sound of her answering laugh, he felt a pang of jealousy that he was not the one who had caused it. When he heard her next remark, he nearly turned around and left.

"Clay, you know I love you—"

Clay interrupted her by clutching his heart dramatically and dropping on his knees in front of her chair.

"Just say the word and I'm all yours. But be gentle. I'm a tender young lad."

Rachel pushed him and he collapsed on his rear in the floor. "As I was saying. I love you—like a brother—and as far as I'm concerned—"

He held up both palms to stop her. "I know, I know. There can never be anything serious between us and I've got to learn to accept that even though it takes away my reason for living." He put his hand over his chest and pretended to faint against the couch. "Nothing can ever mend my broken heart."

Rachel laughed at his antics and outside on the porch Joe heaved a major sigh of relief. The last thing he needed was Clay Cusak's competition.

"Would a banana split from Perkins' Ice Cream Emporium help ease your pain?" she asked.

Clay jumped to his feet, grinning and fully recovered. "It would be a start. Are you buying?"

That was Joe's cue and he tapped on the door, embarrassed by the smug glee he felt at the other man's rejection.

"Mayor Morgan!" Rachel was surprised to see Joe. "What are you doing here?"

"I left my briefcase under my chair this afternoon," he explained through the screen. "May I step around back and get it?"

Clay shouldered Rachel aside and held open the door. "Come on in, Joe. No need to stand out there in the dark."

Rachel glared at Clay. The man was far too hospitable. "I take it you two know each other," she said.

"Sure. Joe and I go back a few years." The two men shook hands.

"Not as far back as you two, evidently." Joe had known that Lydia and Clay's mother, Norma, were friends, but it hadn't occurred to him that Clay might have a crush on Rachel.

Rachel detected something in Joe's tone that she didn't like. If he'd been eavesdropping on her, he'd have to pay. She sidled up to Clay and put her arm around his waist companionably. "Clay's a dear friend. His family lived next door to us for years. We're the same age—our birthdays are just days apart."

"Yeah," Clay put in. "I've seen Rachel naked. Of course, she was only two at the time."

She pinched her friend who yelped in indignation. "We went to kindergarten together and were in the same class right up through junior high."

"My mom worked, so I stayed with the Foxes after school. I've always considered Lydia my other mother. Boy, could she bake."

"After Dad died, Mom moved here because she felt it was safer. Clay's mom was also widowed, so she came a few months later," Rachel added.

Clay took over the narrative. "I was here visiting when I heard Mr. Threadwell was ready to retire and sell the drugstore. I'd just finished pharmacy school and figured this was as good a place as any to hang out my shingle. Would you like to sit down, Joe?"

"He can't stay." Rachel turned to Joe. "You can't stay, can you?"

When Joe realized how uncomfortable Rachel was, he became determined. "I'm in no hurry," he said as he settled on the sofa. He turned to Clay. "I recall that you added new lines of merchandise to the inventory down at the store and extended the hours. That was a smart business move."

"I do okay," he said modestly.

"He does better than okay," Rachel asserted. "He paid off the loan on the place last week."

Clay laughed self-consciously. "You'll have to forgive Rachel. Money stuff impresses the hell out of her."

"So I've discovered."

Rachel stood up and said. "I hate to rush you off, Mayor, but maybe you should go find your briefcase. Clay and I have a date."

Clay perked up, surprised. "We do?"

"Ice cream, remember?"

"Not just ice cream—banana splits. You want to join us, Joe?" Clay asked.

"Well—"

"I'm sure he doesn't even like ice cream," Rachel put in.

It was clear that she did not want his company. For some reason that made Joe even more determined to tag along. "Actually, I love the stuff."

Mrs. Perkins was wiping the counter when they arrived. When the brass bell tinkled over the door, she glanced up. "Evening, folks. Clay Cusak, where have you been? I've been trying to call you for over an hour."

"Contrary to popular opinion, Mrs. Perkins, I do not live behind the counter at the drugstore. I have to go home occasionally, or my landlord gets suspicious."

"Mama's out of her dizzy pills."

Clay smiled at the woman. "She takes that medication in the morning and at bedtime. I have a hunch she knew she'd need it refilled before I closed today."

Mrs. Perkins shrugged. "Well, you know Mama. She runs on her own schedule."

"I'll run down and get them as soon as we have our banana splits. The lady's treating."

"Coming right up. And thanks, Clay." The woman began dipping ice cream into clear glass boats.

They settled at a small table and Joe scooted his chair close to Rachel's. He rested his arm on the back of her chair as he leaned forward to talk to Clay. Her heart fluttered and she felt a warm tingle spread upward to settle in her cheeks. She detested the way her body reacted to his nearness and willed him to take his arm away. But he left it there as if he were totally unaware of the effect he had on her.

Normally, Joe wasn't a touchy-feely person, but it felt so good to be close to Rachel that, for a moment, he considered what it would be like to have the right to touch her anytime he needed to. He quickly put that thought out of his mind.

Mrs. Perkins brought the banana splits and Rachel knew the exact moment when Joe finally took his arm away. She sighed in relief. When he was that close, she felt breathless. She told herself it was because he was so pompous he sucked up all the oxygen. She then turned her full attention on the frozen treat before her while the two men talked.

"So how long have you two been dating?" Joe asked Clay.

Before Clay could reply, Rachel answered, "Oh, years and years. We went to the junior prom together." That was their first and last date and it had occurred primarily because neither of them had been invited by anyone else.

"I gave Rachel her first kiss." The sparkle in Clay's eyes told her he wasn't averse to playing along with the fraud she was perpetrating. "How old were you, honey?"

"Seven," she said tightly.

"Oh, yeah. You punched me in the nose as I recall."

She shot him a glance that said she'd do it again, if he didn't help her out of this. She groaned when he bolted down the last of his banana split and announced cheerfully, "Well, I'd better go get those dizzy pills for Mrs. Perkins's mama. I wouldn't want the old lady to swoon. You don't mind walking Rachel home, do you Joe?"

"Not at all." This couldn't have worked out better if he and Clay had prearranged it.

Clay clapped Joe on the shoulder on his way out and Rachel could swear that there was some kind of good old boy conspiracy going on. She ate her ice cream and said nothing.

"My secretary is expecting a baby," Joe said after a few minutes.

"Congratulations," she replied dryly. "I hope you'll all be very happy."

"It's not mine. Lou Ann and her husband, Jim, want to buy a house. They saw one of your signs over on Mulberry and mentioned they were interested. Maybe you should call them."

This was the first good lead Rachel had had in days. "Why are you being so nice?" she asked suspiciously.

"You're a real-estate broker. They want to buy a house. I guess I just put two and two together."

"Thanks. I'll call them tomorrow."

They looked up when the bell over the door tinkled. "You won't have to call," Joe said. "Here they are now."

After he introduced Rachel to the young couple, she said, "The mayor says you're interested in Mr. White's house."

"Is he asking very much for it?" Lou Ann asked.

"Not really," Rachel replied. "You know he recently married a widow over in Starke. They've decided to live in her house and sell his. He's in a hurry to get it off his hands."

"Can we look at it tomorrow?"

"Sure." Rachel was eager to do business, any business. "What time shall I pick you up?"

"It'll have to be early," Jim said. "I'm playing golf in the morning, then we're going to my folks."

"Can you meet us there at eight, Rachel?" Lou Ann asked.

"I'll be there," Rachel assured her. The three-bedroom house was perfect for Lou Ann and Jim. She'd never been one to lie about in bed in the mornings, so it would be no hardship to show them the property. Her mother usually slept until nine. At her physical therapist's urging, Lydia was becoming more independent in her morning routine.

After the couple got their ice-cream cones and left, Rachel looked at Joe speculatively. "Thanks for the lead, Mayor."

"Don't mention it."

They didn't talk much on the walk home. When they arrived, Joe turned to Rachel. "I'll just get my briefcase and get out of your way. I know you didn't want to spend the evening with me."

"You shouldn't have butted in," she said as she followed him through the side gate. The only light came from the half-moon, and the night air was warm and thick with the perfume of flowers. Mrs. Puddleduck squawked in her pen, but Rachel told Joe to ignore her.

Joe found his briefcase right where he'd left it, but made no move to leave.

"I know I shouldn't have forced my company on you tonight, but when I saw you with Clay I got jealous." Confession was supposed to be good for the soul.

"You have no right to be jealous of me."

"I know I don't. But I can't control my feelings."

"I don't know why not. I do."

How well he knew that. "You never did tell me what you have against me. Other than besting you fair and square in a business deal, I haven't done anything to you."

"And you're not going to. Ever." She pretended complete indifference even as he stepped up behind her.

"I can't decide whether you're afraid of me or yourself," he whispered.

He was so close, she could feel his breath in her hair. "I'm not afraid of anything."

He slipped one hand beneath the heavy fall of her hair and caressed her nape. "Why are you so tense?"

"I am not tense." How could he think she was tense when every bone in her body seemed to dissolve at his touch?

He lifted her hair and nibbled the back of her neck. "When are you going to stop fighting it and admit that there's something between us?"

She wanted to wrench away from him, but his warm lips sent a delightful shiver down her spine. "Never."

"Never say never," he whispered.

"Now you sound like my mother." She worked up the strength to move away from him. "Stop slobbering on my neck."

"Why?"

"Because I don't like the way you make me feel."

"Yes, you do. Maybe you aren't scared of anything, but you scare the hell out of me."

"I won't take advantage of that fact, if you won't."

Joe grinned. Rachel was the most fascinating woman he'd ever encountered. Whether she was right for him or not, she'd gotten under his skin. "So you admit that something is happening here?"

"Okay. I admit it. Are you satisfied now?"

"Not by a long shot."

Her heart pumped fiercely when he turned her in his arms. She tipped back her head and opened her lips with a sigh. There was something utterly sensual about this man that banished good sense. His nearness made her reckless and she yearned for his kiss.

Joe wrapped her in his arms and pulled her close. His lips covered hers in a teasing caress that made her arch against him in a silent plea for more. One hand cupped the back of her head and threaded through the silk of her hair, while the other tested the swell of her breast. His tongue delved between her parted lips to savor her warmth.

She moaned softly as he stroked her breast with his thumb and Joe was startled by the powerful sensations threatening his own control. Her hands were inside his jacket, roaming his back, and he groaned with pleasure when she pressed her tongue into his mouth.

Rachel forgot the enmity she felt for this man. She was aware only of her overloaded senses registering the cool fire of Joe's lips on hers, the spicy fragrance of his soap, the unbearable need his touch aroused. His kiss was gentle, yet commanding. Sobering, yet intoxicating. It made her feel soft and vulnerable and hopelessly at the mercy of his unyielding body.

Reluctantly, Joe lifted his head. He wanted the kiss to go on forever and that very feeling made him end it. Never had he felt so threatened by his own emotions.

Rachel squirmed out of his arms and stepped away. "I wish you hadn't done that."

"If you tell me you didn't enjoy it, I'll call you a liar."

"I think it would be wise if we didn't pursue this."

"Are we going to be wise?" He wanted to touch her so badly that he attempted to take her in his arms again.

"I don't see why not," she said as she sidestepped his embrace. "We're both adults."

"Consenting adults," he reminded her.

"Not that consenting. Face it. You don't want a future with me any more than I want one with you."

"I don't know what I want. Hell, I barely know you. All I know is that when I'm near you, I want you so much, it makes me crazy." Joe had hoped that being alone with her would help him sort out his feelings. It had only muddled his thinking.

"We shouldn't get everything we want. I once wanted the chicken pox so I could stay home from school and be coddled and catered to like Molly. I got my wish and I was so miserable, I couldn't stop scratching. I'll never forget that itch. I still have the scars. Sometimes the things we want are bad for us."

"Are you comparing me with plague and pestilence?" Joe asked.

"Believe me, you don't want that kind of itch. Better to avoid the source."

"That'll be hard to do. Morgan's Point is a small town."

"I won't be around forever. You can surely control your caveman instincts for a few more weeks."

"I forgot. You're just slumming here. When your mother's well enough, you'll be going back to your real life."

"That's right. I can't wait."

"Fine. Just don't hang around trying to weasel a deal on Cypress Knoll. We don't want your kind of development here."

"A lawyer calling me a weasel. That's a good one."

"Maybe it would be best for everyone if you went back to the city." Joe was losing patience with this conversation. Things hadn't turned out at all like he'd planned.

"And maybe it would be best if you left right now," she said vehemently.

He snatched up his briefcase and stalked away. A woman couldn't make it any plainer than that. "No need to see me out."

Rachel went to bed, but it was very late before she finally fell asleep. Even then, dreams of Joe Morgan intruded upon her rest. That's why she overslept the next morning and was running late when she left for her appointment. No problem, she thought with a glance at her watch. If she hurried, she could still make it in time.

She cursed under her breath when the flashing light on the police car signaled her to pull over just after she turned off Main Street. "What's wrong, Officer?" she asked as the uniformed policeman approached. She'd seen him around town but couldn't recall his name. "I'm in a hurry."

"So I noticed," he said as he walked up to her car window. "Nice car. BMW, isn't it?"

"Yes, it is. I'd love to chat, but I really don't have time. I'm supposed to meet Jim and Lou Ann Boyd at Mr. White's house in four minutes."

"In that case, I'll move right along. May I see your license, your verification of insurance and your automobile registration, please?"

"What for?"

"So I can give you your speeding ticket and you can be on your way," he said as he flipped open his citation book. She glanced at the name tag on his uniform. Hacker. "Speeding ticket?"

He nodded as he wrote in his book. "You were going twenty-five in a fifteen-mile-an-hour zone."

"You're kidding!"

"Nope. I clocked you."

"My car won't go fifteen miles an hour. It idles faster than that," she protested sarcastically.

"You might want to take it down to Harley's Garage and have the timing checked," he suggested.

"There's nothing wrong with my timing." At least not the mechanical kind. Rachel shuddered at the thought of Harley Smith's grease-stained hands touching the cream-colored leather interior. "Besides, the speed limit in this town is twenty-five."

"In most areas. But the residential streets are fifteen miles an hour between 6:00 a.m. and 9:00 a.m. on Tuesdays, Thursdays and Saturdays."

"That's ridiculous."

"It dates back to when Fred Zimmerman used to deliver ice in a horse-drawn wagon."

"Pardon me?"

"Fred had this old nag named Cleta who was real spooky. When cars whizzed past her going twenty-five, she'd buck and snort and upset the wagon, blocking traffic and causing no end of trouble. Fred would be late delivering the ice and the housewives would be mad because their iceboxes warmed up."

"When the cars whizzed past?" Rachel repeated.

"That's right. It was determined that twenty-five miles per hour constituted a careless disregard for public safety. The town council passed an ordinance to make the speed limit fifteen miles an hour on delivery days so Fred and Cleta could do their job."

Rachel was still taking it in. "What year was that ordinance passed, Officer Hacker?"

He scratched his chin. "I don't know exactly, but it was probably sometime in the twenties. I believe Fred retired in '33."

"Oh, so he's not delivering ice by wagon anymore? He and Cleta?"

"Oh, no, ma'am. Cleta got sunstroked and dropped dead in the traces one day. Fred's heart really wasn't in it after that."

"So basically, what you're telling me is that the speed limit has been obsolete for sixty years."

"It's still on the books," he insisted. "So it's still the law."

She looked around. "It's not posted."

"The signs fell down a long time ago. Everybody knows the law, so they weren't replaced."

"Do you think it's fair to give me a ticket when I wasn't aware of the ordinance?" she asked in a placating manner.

"Ignorance of the law is no excuse," he pointed out. "The law's the law and I'm sworn to uphold it." He tore off the ticket and handed her a copy. "If I were you, I wouldn't be so careless in the future."

"I intend to protest this. It amounts to legal highway robbery."

"It won't do you a bit of good to protest. The law applies equally to everyone in Morgan's Point, resident or visitor."

"Did the mayor put you up to this?" Rachel asked suspiciously. This sounded like something Morgan would do.

"The mayor has his job, I have mine."

Rachel narrowed her gaze. "He did, didn't he?"

"I can't say that he did."

"And you won't say that he didn't." Rachel snatched the ticket out of the officer's hand and blanched when she looked at it. "Fifty dollars! This *is* highway robbery and I'm not so sure now that it is legal."

"It is in Morgan's Point."

She fumed. "You tell Mayor Morgan I'll be talking to him later."

"If I see him, I'll sure tell him. But it's Saturday, so he's probably at home. I guess it can wait 'til Monday."

"I'll just tell him myself." She had no intention of waiting until Monday to protest Joe Morgan's little revenue-generating speed trap. By Monday, she'd have time to cool down. She fully intended to see him today while she was still boiling hot.

Chapter Four

Rachel decided to cancel her appointment with Lou Ann and Jim and drive straight to Morgan's house to have it out with him. She was convinced that he had instructed Officer Hacker to cite her for speeding.

Speeding! Only someone still living in the horse-and-buggy days would consider twenty-five miles per hour careless. Not only was Morgan chauvinistic, he was old-fashioned. He admitted he thought a woman's place was in the home; he probably believed wives should be barefoot and pregnant, as well.

The truth was, he was angry because she had rebuffed his advances. Maybe he could fool some people, her mother included, but she wasn't about to be buffaloed by his boy-next-door good looks. Or by his winning, annoying, charm. No doubt he was unaccustomed to women telling him they weren't interested.

Well, she wasn't. Not by a long shot. And she'd reiterate her disinterest when she confronted him about abusing the authority of his office in such a blatant manner. She'd longed to find a chink in his armor of perfection and she'd finally found it. Corruption was such a wonderful chink!

While she waited impatiently at a red light, the rational part of her brain, the part concerned with business and income, protested her impulsive behavior. In the end, logic prevailed over temper. She couldn't afford to cancel her appointment. Lou Ann and her husband were genuinely interested in that house and she had a professional responsibility to show it to them. She also had a burning need to negotiate a deal. Any deal. All this relaxing and avoiding stress was giving her an ulcer.

When the light changed, she made a U-turn in the middle of the deserted street and headed back the way she'd come. She could deal with Joe Morgan later. Right now she wouldn't allow him to cost her another sale.

She'd gone less than a block when she heard the dreaded squeal of the siren. With a groan, she pulled over and glanced in the rearview mirror to see the familiar hulking form of Officer Hacker approach from his black-and-white patrol car.

"I didn't expect to see you again so soon," he said with grim pleasure as he pulled out his citation book and flipped it open.

"Let me guess," Rachel said through clenched teeth. "It's illegal to make a U-turn on this street when the second Saturday of the month coincides with the new moon cycle in a leap year."

The patrolman eyed her sternly; he obviously had no sense of the absurd. Apparently sarcasm would get her nowhere with Mr. Law and Order.

"It's illegal to make a U-turn on this street anytime," he told her. "It constitutes a—"

"Careless disregard for public safety," she finished for him.

"Actually, city ordinance defines an illegal U-turn as a *reckless* disregard for public safety," he informed her as he scribbled on his pad. "It's a more serious offense."

She released a long, disgruntled breath. "From careless to reckless. At least I'm moving up in the crime world."

"This is no laughing matter, miss. Such dangerous maneuvers could result in a serious accident."

She glanced around and the only thing afoot was a twitchy-tailed squirrel in hot pursuit of brunch. "You know, Officer, now that you've pointed it out to me, I can see the potential disaster of crossing the path of an out-of-control rodent."

Officer Hacker finally smiled as he handed out her second ticket of the morning. Two tickets! Why, she hadn't even had that many cups of coffee.

"I'm just doing my job, ma'am. The—"

"I know. The law's the law." She wasn't at all surprised when she saw that the fine was sixty dollars. After all, it was only natural that reckless disregard should cost the miscreant more than mere carelessness did.

Rachel stuffed the ticket into her purse. "Let me ask you something. Does this town need a new bridge or maybe a water treatment plant?"

"Not that I know of. Why?"

"I thought maybe the mayor was planning to finance new public works by having you follow me around all day issuing tickets for every little infraction."

Again, her sarcasm eluded him. "Does that mean you're planning to break some more laws today, miss?"

She supposed that murder would be considered a felony here. Murdering the mayor was probably a hanging offense. "No, I plan to curtail my wanton crime spree long enough to tell Mayor Morgan exactly what I think of him and his outdated, outmoded and outrageous traffic laws." Rachel's logical mind gave her the cerebral equivalent of a poke in the ribs. "Just as soon as I close a deal, that is."

Officer Hacker tipped his hat. "Drive carefully now, miss, and have a nice day."

That would be impossible. Any day Rachel received two tickets and tangled with Joe Morgan was sure to be unpleasant.

As it turned out, Lou Ann and Jim were half an hour late for their appointment. Rachel spent the time constructively—pacing the sidewalk in front of Mr. White's house and plotting revenge against the illustrious mayor. It wasn't even 9:00 a.m. and already his antiquated laws had cost her over a hundred dollars. Not that she was going to pay those trumped-up citations.

Once Morgan realized that she wasn't going to swoon in his arms, he wanted her out of his precious town. He was afraid people would start listening to her and decide to sell Cypress Knoll out from under him. If he thought annoyance tactics would drive her back to Jacksonville, he was wrong. However, if he was trying to provoke her, he was succeeding. Beyond his wildest dreams.

He'd made her mad and he'd live to regret it. MegaMont was history, but that didn't mean there weren't others who would be interested in his sacred piece of dirt. She'd beat the bushes until she found a deal the council of Morgan's Point couldn't refuse. Then she'd see who'd have the last laugh.

When her prospective clients finally showed up, Rachel gave them a tour of the house. They liked it, but wanted to think about it before making an offer. The delay denied Rachel the emotional release of consummating a sale, but it allowed her to maintain a full head of steam when she pounded on Morgan's door fifteen minutes later.

He took his time answering and as she waited, she glanced around in irritation. The yard was well kept and studded with bright flowers. A gnarled old tree shaded the front porch. The house was at least a hundred years old, but it wasn't showing its age. The exterior was painted a rich country blue and the wide porch and railings gleamed white in the morning sun. Huge baskets of Boston ferns swung gently in the arches created by the gingerbread woodwork of the veranda, and pots of red geraniums lined the steps.

It had the confidence that only a house which has stood a very long time can have. Its sturdy clapboard and neat shutters said, *I was here before you and I'll be here after you're gone.* Despite its air of superiority, it was a welcoming, homey place, full of warmth and charm.

It irritated Rachel that Joe Morgan lived there. He belonged in a cave like the Neanderthal he was.

When Joe answered the door, he seemed genuinely surprised to see her, but Rachel didn't believe it for a moment. She was sure he'd already received a full report of her criminal activities from his coconspirator, Officer Hacker.

"Rachel! How nice of you to drop by." Considering the way their conversation had ended last night, Joe was amazed to see her standing on his front porch. "Won't you come in?"

"No, thank you. What I have to say can be said from right here." She backed up a few steps and tried not to notice how attractive he looked in his baggy khaki pants and Saturday stubble. He was wearing an old-fashioned undershirt, the sleeveless kind favored by elderly men. However, Joe didn't look like anybody's grandpa. His firm brown muscles contrasted nicely with the snowy white cotton.

Joe had no idea what she was talking about and waited for her to state her business. If body language was all it was cracked up to be, someone had recently crossed her. He felt sorry for the misguided soul foolish enough to engage in a contest of wills with the queen of fire and ice.

"Sit down on the glider and I'll bring you a cup of tea."

"I don't want any tea. I want to know what you propose to do about these." She thrust the tickets at him.

Joe looked the citations over carefully before speaking. "Do you want me to represent you in court?"

She snorted. "Not hardly."

His eyes narrowed as he returned the papers to her. "I hope you aren't expecting me to fix these tickets, Rachel. Because if that's what you're after, I'm afraid I can't help you."

"I suppose your principles won't allow you to abuse the power of your office in such a despicable way."

"No, they won't."

"Don't give me that. I know you put Hacker up to this. My God, he followed me around all morning just waiting for me to sneeze in a no-parking zone."

Joe was confused. He was being blamed for something, but he wasn't quite sure what. "I'm afraid I don't understand."

"You know darn well what I'm talking about. You didn't like me giving you the brush-off last night and you got your revenge by siccing Robocop on me."

Understanding finally dawned on Joe. "Am I supposed to be angry and vengeful because you rejected my attentions?" he asked with strained amusement.

"I wouldn't put it past you."

"Don't flatter yourself, Ms. Fox. Not only am I not responsible for your tickets, I haven't given you a single thought since I left your house last night."

That last detail wasn't exactly true, but knowing how intensely he had been thinking of her would only give Rachel the upper hand. He knew from experience not to relinquish even the smallest advantage; he'd need every one he could get.

He watched her expression of hostility change subtly into a combination of chagrin and indignation. "Are you saying that you didn't order Officer Hacker to harrass me?"

"I did not." Joe considered himself self-reliant. "If I felt there was any harrassing to do, I would do it myself."

Rachel was momentarily taken aback, and for the first time since he'd known her, she seemed speechless. Joe seized the opportunity to loose one more zinger. "Either you have overestimated your charm, or you have underestimated my principles."

"Are you always this pompous in the morning, or do you have to work at it like some people work at lowering their cholesterol level?" she demanded.

Joe was tired of the verbal sparring. It was much too early for thinking on his feet. "Oh, for Pete's sake, Rachel. Sit down and shut up for a few minutes. You probably haven't noticed, but it's a beautiful day. There's not a cloud in the sky, a cool breeze is blowing in from the coast and there's a hummingbird in the hibiscus. Why don't you relax and enjoy life once in a while instead of always running around with your sword drawn?''

This confrontation wasn't turning out as she'd planned. In her confusion, Rachel allowed herself to be pushed down onto the colorfully striped glider, her pride still stinging from his remarks. Could it be true that the tickets weren't his fault? Joe Morgan was many things, but she didn't think he was a liar. Stubborn, chauvinistic and old-fashioned maybe, but not a liar. He exuded integrity from every pore.

She supposed it was possible that Officer Hacker was just a particularly zealous and dedicated patrolman. If that were the case, she'd made a fool of herself by coming here and making false accusations. Now if she could get out gracefully.

"Just sit there," he ordered as though divining her thoughts. "Don't say a word. Be quiet and enjoy the tranquillity." When she started to protest, he interrupted. "I said, be quiet. You'll frighten my hummingbird. I'm going inside for tea and you'd better be here when I get back. I'm tired of always fighting with you. It's time we talked."

He turned at the doorway and looked at her with mock sternness. "If you're not here when I return, I'll have to see if Officer Hacker wants to cite you for leaving the scene of a crime."

Joe disappeared into the house and Rachel sat in the glider and fumed. She pushed the swing back and forth at a furious pace, torn between staying and telling him exactly what she thought of him, and leaving him to figure it out on his own. Morgan had no right to tell her what to do. If she wanted to go, she'd go. She was a busy woman, she couldn't sit around all day watching hummingbirds. She had things to do, people to see. A moment wasted was a dollar lost in her business. Besides, if she hung around, she'd eventually have to apologize to Morgan for thinking the worst of him.

She couldn't do that. Not when she wanted to think the worst of him.

She was still vacillating when Joe returned with two mugs of fragrant tea. He handed one to her and sat down beside her on the glider. "Isn't it amazing? His tiny wings beat so rapidly that the movement is just a blur."

Rachel scooted as far away from him as she could. "Whose tiny wings are you referring to?"

"The ruby-throated hummingbird."

"Oh, him. Yeah, it's amazing all right."

"I forgot. You aren't interested in nature."

"No, I'm not. I don't trust animals. I think they should all be in zoos where somebody can keep an eye on them."

She hadn't meant to be funny, but he laughed. "Surely you appreciate the fresh air and peace and quiet of Morgan's Point."

"Peace and quiet gives me a headache and fresh air makes me sneeze," she said distractedly.

"You're having a worse time adjusting to small-town life than I thought."

"I don't know what you're talking about."

"You view life as some kind of contest, Rachel," he speculated. "Whoever has the fullest appointment book when he dies is the winner."

"Very funny."

"Things move at a different pace here," he pointed out unnecessarily.

"So I noticed," she replied dryly. "Any town where driving twenty-five miles per hour constitutes a disregard for public safety, is not only moving at a different pace, it's moving in a parallel universe."

"When you're in Rome, you're supposed to do as the Romans do," he reminded her.

"Then I'd best be moseyin' over to the general store for a stimulatin' game of bottle-cap checkers," she said in an exaggerated drawl as she started to rise.

He made her sit down again. "Don't belittle a life-style you don't understand, Rachel. People here are happy with small pleasures. We have a strong sense of history and deep feelings for the land. I know you don't understand that, but I can't believe you're such a narrow-minded snob that you won't even try to see a different point of view."

"Who are you calling a narrow-minded snob?" she demanded.

"You."

No one had ever accused her of that before. She'd been called opinionated and cynical, determined and ambitious, and other such terms of grudging admiration by business rivals. But no one had ever called her narrow-minded. And never, ever, a snob.

"I resent that, Morgan."

"Then prove otherwise."

"I don't have to prove anything. As I recall, you and I are declared enemies."

"And why is that? Because I love Morgan's Point and you don't give a damn about it or its people? Because I don't want to see my town turned into a tasteless tourist trap full of minimalls and factory outlet stores so you and others who don't care can make a few bucks?"

"Because you can't see beyond your own nose. You won't accept the fact that if someone doesn't breathe some economic life into this town, it's going to die."

"Morgan's Point is doing just fine."

"Someone needs to bring it into the twentieth century."

"And you're just the person to do that, huh? You've been here, what? Two whole weeks? Already you're an expert on what's good for Morgan's Point."

"You can't stand in the way of progress, Morgan."

"I can, if it means disaster," he said resolutely.

"Do you think you have a genetic responsibility for this town just because your great-great-great-grandfather founded it?"

"He, and others like him, carved it out of the wilderness. Morgan's Point has survived wars and natural disasters. It can survive a plague of profit-minded real-estate developers whose only goal is making money. Even if it means destroying the beauty of the area in the process."

"You've been watching too much television, Morgan. Not all developers are sharks out to consume everything in their paths. MegaMont wasn't planning to come in with bulldozers and chainsaws to clear-cut everything in sight."

"Weren't they?"

"If you'd ever acknowledge the twentieth century, you'd realize that there are ecologically sound methods of development that preserve the integrity of the land."

"I've heard of that. If you have time, we can drive over to Sinola and I can show you ecologically sound building methods in action."

"What's Sinola?"

"It's a town about fifty miles south of here. Five years ago, some hotshot came in and convinced the people they needed progress. He claimed, as you put it, that he could breathe some economic life into the community. Maybe you should see the results of that resuscitation. Of course, it'll mean calling a temporary truce."

Rachel glanced at her watch. "I don't know. I have a lot to do today."

"Name one thing."

Damn him for knowing that she had nothing but time on her hands. In a town where most of the citizens were third- or fourth-generation residents, her "work" consisted mainly of waiting around for the telephone to ring and dreaming of all the deals she was missing out on in Jacksonville. Managing the local branch office of Fox Realty provided the intellectual stimulation of baby-sitting a pet rock.

"I need to check on Mother."

"She can come along. We can stop somewhere for lunch and make a day of it."

"I don't think so."

Joe was frustrated by her reluctance to spend a few hours with him. "For Pete's sake, Rachel, I don't bite. If it'll make you happy, we won't stop for lunch. We won't talk about anything personal and I promise we won't enjoy ourselves. We can continue to be downright nasty to each other."

"It'll just be business?" she asked hesitantly.

"Strictly business. A wonderful opportunity for you to exercise your cynicism. Is that more to your liking?"

Rachel didn't think it was a good idea, but her ego still throbbed from that jab about her being a snob. "All right. But I'm only going so I can view some property."

"I never thought for a moment that it was because you enjoy my company."

"Just so we're straight on that."

"I need to change and shave. I'll pick you and Lydia up in an hour."

Joe smiled, feeling magnanimous. He told her he felt it was time to do something about those outdated traffic laws. He would put them on the agenda for the next council meeting.

She agreed and as Joe watched her walk to her car he wondered why he found Rachel Fox so damn fascinating. Her matter-of-fact beauty was part of it, but there was more to it than that. She was the most stubborn, opinionated and ill-suited woman he'd ever met. They had nothing in common and were destined to butt heads on every issue that arose. There was no future in cultivating a friendship or anything else with her.

So why was he wasting his time?

As he turned and went into the house, Joe found an answer he could live with. Since he was too smart to want to get involved with Rachel, maybe what he wanted was to find out what made her tick so he could stop her. Now that she was living in Morgan's Point, she'd be peddling her progressive viewpoint to all who would listen.

What's more, her mother was well liked and people had been sympathetic since her unfortunate accident. Rather than viewing Rachel as the meddlesome outsider she was, some considered her a selfless heroine who had willingly placed her career on hold to care for her poor, injured mother.

Altruistic she might be, but Joe knew Rachel was not about to miss the main chance. Her self-imposed exile in Morgan's Point was a perfect opportunity to further her career and make a pile of money at the same time. If she could create enough interest in the sale of Cypress Knoll to bring the issue up for a vote, he might have a real battle on his hands. A battle he was determined to win. He would yet see the wilderness area turned into a protected wildlife refuge.

He convinced himself that it wasn't Rachel he was interested in. He only wanted to protect Morgan's Point from her brand of progress. There were two ways to do that: he could fight her, or he could change her mind and make her see his point of view. It was a well-known fact that one could catch more flies with honey than with vinegar.

There was nothing wrong with trying to teach the strong-willed Ms. Fox that she couldn't fight city hall.

Chapter Five

"What do you mean you can't go?" Rachel followed her mother from room to room as the older woman got ready for the day. "You have to go."

"I'm going to a country auction with Ernie," Lydia explained.

"You don't even like auctions."

"The old me never did, but the new me loves them," she said with a wave of her hand.

Rachel shuddered at the thought of her absentminded mother bidding good money on God-only-knew-what. "Maybe I should go with you."

"No, thank you. You might need a chaperon on your dates, Rachel, but I'm quite old enough to take care of myself."

"I am not having a date with Joe Morgan," she clarified insistently.

"Of course you're not." Lydia smiled. "You're just going to view some property. It's just business."

"Exactly."

Lydia smiled again. "Exactly."

"If you're not going, I'm not going." Rachel folded her arms and leaned against the doorjamb. "I can't go tearing off into the hinterlands alone with that man."

"I can't think of anyone I'd rather go tearing off with, if I were twenty-five years younger."

"Mother, be serious."

"I am serious. I don't know what's wrong with you, Rachel. Joe Morgan is one of the nicest young men I know."

"He is not! He's stubborn and unreasonable."

"Like I said before, dear, it's good to have a few things in common."

"Mother!"

"Just go, Rachel. Relax and get to know Joe. You'd like him if you'd give him half a chance."

"I don't want to like him," she muttered.

Lydia pulled on a wide-brimmed hat just as a car horn sounded outside. "Gotta go. There's Ernie." She kissed her daughter on the forehead as she went by. "Have fun in the hinterlands, dear."

Rachel felt deserted. Fun? How could she have fun when she and Joe Morgan disagreed on too many things to ever find a common ground? Maybe he was physically attractive, but he was not her type and never would be. With that thought firmly in mind, she went into the living room, looked up his phone number and dialed his house. It wasn't too late to get out of this.

Her foot tapped impatiently as she listened to the phone ring at the other end. It hadn't been an hour already, had it? "Answer, dammit," she willed under her breath.

Joe lifted the brass knocker and tapped twice. Rachel had made it clear that this was no more than a business appointment, but he felt nervous all the same. He still didn't understand why she had that effect on him, but it didn't matter. His goal was to change her mind about Cypress Knoll.

"You're early," she said when she opened the door.

"Is that a problem?"

"I guess not," she said grudgingly.

He extended a large, freshly cut bouquet, hoping she would accept his clumsy attempt at a peace offering.

"What's that?" she asked unnecessarily.

Joe stared at the bouquet, which had seemed like a good idea when he'd cut it from his garden. Why was he even trying to get along with this exasperating woman? "Flowers."

"I can see that," she said impatiently. "Flowers are such a typical male response."

"Excuse me for being male," he said, his frustration showing.

Rachel wasn't sure why the sight of Joe Morgan with a handful of posies upset her so much. Normally, she liked getting flowers. Loved it, in fact. She just didn't want to get flowers from him. "Did you think a few blossoms would soften me up and win you points?"

"A welding torch couldn't soften you up," he muttered. Thinking fast, he rallied to save face. "Actually, I brought them for your mother."

"Oh." Rachel didn't like the way he made her feel. "Mother's not here. She's out for the day. I'll put them in water."

"Then she won't be going with us?"

She carried the flowers into the kitchen. "Unfortunately, no." They'd be all alone.

Joe pointed out various landmarks as they drove through Morgan's Point. When she mentioned that the architecture and street design looked more New England than Southern, he explained that it was because many of the early settlers had come from that part of the country, including the Morgans who had immigrated from New Hampshire.

The business district was designed around a bustling old-fashioned square with a small, tree-shaded park in the center. The sidewalks in front of the quaint stores and shops were wide and well swept. No parking was allowed on the main square and foot traffic predominated.

A whitewashed bandstand was the focal point of the park. Over the years, it had been the scene of political debates, free concerts and even a few weddings. According to Joe, it would soon be hung with bunting and bows in anticipation of the Chamber Follies, a local fundraising event that had become a tradition.

It was Saturday morning and streets were busy. Rachel knew from her mother that locals timed their shopping trips to coincide with their neighbors'. That way they could meet for lunch at the Calico Cat Tea Room or enjoy a little gossip while taking a breather in the shade of the park.

"Three years ago, the Follies raised enough money to install the Victorian street lamps on the square," Joe told her.

"They're very quaint." The place had potential. Add a few more restaurants, some art galleries and a couple of bed-and-breakfasts, and the tourists would come.

When she said as much to Joe, he responded, "Many of the families here go back generations. Folks don't take to outsiders coming in and changing things."

Rachel suspected he was voicing his own opinion. Surely the whole town wasn't full of unreasonable and unprogressive people. Several waved at them as they passed and most greeted Joe by name. Two old men sitting on a bench in front of the barbershop saluted.

"Morgan's Pointers seem friendly enough," Rachel observed.

"We all know each other. We're all friends."

That was the problem. In Morgan's Point, everybody knew everybody, their business and their perversities. Rachel wasn't accustomed to so much friendliness. Or so much warmth. Instead of comforting her, the personal interest of total strangers made her nervous. You couldn't have secrets in this town because your life was an open and well-read book.

Passing a tumbledown old building on the edge of town, Joe slowed his Jeep so that Rachel could get a better look at it.

"That's the oldest brick schoolhouse in the county," he told her. "It dates back to the mid-1800s."

"It's a wreck," she pointed out.

"It needs some restoration work," he admitted.

"Some?" she asked with a laugh.

"Okay, it needs a lot. I've established a fund for that purpose, but it's slow-going."

"Possibly because sane people don't want to donate money to a lost cause," she said.

"It needs to be preserved."

"What it needs is to be torn down."

"But the building has genuine historical significance," he insisted.

"So erect a nice, neat historical marker on the spot where it once stood."

He shook his head. "You don't have any sense of history, do you, Rachel?"

"History has its place. For example, I love St. Augustine," she said, referring to a popular coastal town. "It's the oldest permanent European settlement in the continental United States and just brimful of history."

"What do you like about it?" he wanted to know as he turned the Jeep onto a back road. He'd explained that they weren't taking the main highway to Sinola. He claimed the scenery was more interesting along the less-traveled route.

She considered his question. "I like the Arts and Crafts Spring Festival. And the Parade of Horses and Carriages on Easter Sunday. The horses look so cute in their Easter hats. And I love the shops and restaurants. And the Great Chowder Debate."

"As interesting as those things are, none of them have much to do with St. Augustine's colorful history."

"They don't?"

"No, they don't. What about the Castillo de San Marcos? Or the Mission of Nombre de Dios? You probably don't know it, but it was the site of the first Mass said in the New World."

"That's nice, but there's no money in old churches. Tourists may take a few pictures of the fort and the mission, but they really go to St. Augustine for the atmosphere, the shopping and the food." When she heard his "Hmmph" beside her, she pressed her argument. "They'd come to Morgan's Point, too, if you gave them something to come for besides ratty old buildings."

He shook his head and drove on. Why did he think he could change Rachel Fox's mind? The woman had a cash register instead of a heart. After he'd driven a few more miles, he pulled the Jeep over to the side of the road, stopped and pointed to the west. "See that tall oak tree over there?"

She had no trouble spotting it since it was one of the few oaks around. Most of the trees in the heavily wooded area were pine and cypress. "What about it?"

"It's called the Trader's Oak. It was already a landmark in the area when Micajah Morgan established the first trading post nearby in 1835."

"Micajah Morgan? That would be your great-great-great-grandfather?"

"Yes. The trading post began as a blanket spread on the ground to display goods, but it eventually became a settlement and finally the town of Morgan's Point. Before there was a courthouse, trials were held under that tree. A few men were even hung from its branches."

"Instant frontier justice," she commented.

"Exactly."

Joe became animated when he talked about Morgan's Point and his ancestors' role in its history. His handsome face lit up in his enthusiasm and he looked younger when he wasn't scowling. Younger and more vulnerable. Try as she would, it was hard to dislike someone who cared as much about things as Joe did.

She tried to imagine what it would be like to be tied to a place by blood and history. She wanted to understand what it meant to look out each day at the same scenery your ancestors had looked at over a hundred years ago. She wanted to, but she couldn't. For too many years, she had viewed property with an eye to its negotiable value. She couldn't afford to get sentimental about it now.

"Who owns the tree?" she asked curiously.

"The town does. It's part of the Cypress Knoll property."

Rachel glanced around with a practiced eye. Now that she thought about it, Trader's Oak would be a wonderful focal point for the development. Trader's Oak Mall, Trader's Oak Inn, Trader's Oak Estates. It had a solid ring to it. The tree itself could stand at the entrance, with a nice marker to commemorate its past. Tourists loved stuff like that and were willing to drive miles out of their way so long as there were accomodations and commercial zones nearby.

"Don't set your greedy designs on Cypress Knoll just yet," Joe said as if reading her mind.

"I don't know what you're talking about," she said innocently.

"Then why do I see dollar signs in your eyes?"

"I was just considering potential," she defended.

"You'll never get Cypress Knoll, so you might as well forget it," he said adamantly.

"Maybe you don't want to sell, but you don't have the last word," she reminded him. "Once I get a firm offer to take back to the town council, I'm sure the more forward-thinking citizens of Morgan's Point will see things my way."

"Don't hold your breath," he muttered.

She said nothing and they rode along in silence for several minutes. Finally, out of the blue, he asked, "Do you ever do anything besides work?"

She looked at him strangely. "Of course."

"Like what?"

"Lots of things," she answered evasively.

"Do you have friends?"

"I certainly do."

"A best girlfriend with whom you talk on the phone for hours, sharing your deepest secrets?" he probed.

"I don't have time to talk on the phone for hours unless it's business."

"You don't have any women friends," he declared. "I
figured you were a loner."

"Why do you say that?"

"Women get to know each other by revealing things
about themselves. You'd never do that."

"And men get acquainted by watching football games
together, drinking beer and belching," she snapped.

"It's a holdover from the caveman days."

"Well, you should know all about that."

"The males of the band hunted together, sitting quietly for hours at a time, waiting for game. It was early
male bonding. Females, on the other hand, spent their
time gathering food and caring for children, all in a group
so they'd have protection. According to some experts,
that early need to gossip may have led to the development of language."

"I didn't know you were a linguist," she said sarcastically.

"I read. Don't you?"

"Yes, I read."

"What?"

"The *Wall Street Journal*, real-estate listings. The
newspaper."

He smiled as though he'd made a point. "Do you have
any hobbies?"

"Heavens, no. Hobbies aren't productive. I don't
waste time on things that don't teach me something,
make me money or..." Her voice trailed off.

"Or what?" he asked.

She'd been about to say, "...or give me pleasure." But
somehow, talking about pleasure with Joe Morgan
seemed like a bad idea.

"Or what?" he demanded.

"None of your business, Morgan. You promised we wouldn't get personal, so just drive."

Joe made no further attempt at small talk and turned up the car radio to a volume that precluded conversation. He'd thought he could reach Rachel and eventually show her why it was so important to preserve Cypress Knoll. Of course, that thought had been predicated on the assumption that she had feelings, that underneath her tough exterior, she had a heart. Now he wasn't so sure. He was tempted to turn the Jeep around and drive her home, but he had to try to get her to give up on the development idea. If a visit to Sinola didn't do it, nothing would.

Before long, the pine and cypress forest gave way to small, carefully marked residential lots. Trees had been cleared in a haphazard manner with little regard for aesthetics. The denuded areas had the look of hastily sutured wounds, since there had been no attempt at relandscaping. There wasn't much grass because the ground was covered with a thick bed of pine needles.

Most of the lots contained battened-down mobile homes with attached porches and awnings, a type of residence favored by retirees on fixed incomes and by those wanting inexpensive summer homes. Colorful plaster lawn ornaments were the primary form of outdoor decor.

"This is the outskirts of Sinola," he told her. "We'll be getting into town in a few minutes."

Rachel had guessed they were coming to a town. Large, garish signs announced everything from sporting goods stores to seafood restaurants to motels for only twenty-one dollars per night. The billboards jostled for space along the roadside, as though vying for their fair share of the tourist dollar.

"Unlike Morgan's Point, Sinola doesn't have a sign ordinance," he explained. "The reason you don't see clutter like this in our town is because we don't allow it. We don't need it, either, since we're not after the tourist trade."

Joe maneuvered the Jeep around a curve in the road and the town of Sinola was laid out in full view. Gas stations and minimarts predominated, along with fast-food restaurants of every persuasion. The business district was nearly deserted, despite the fact that it was Saturday morning. Many of the storefronts were vacant, with graffitti scrawled over their boarded-up windows.

"Where is everyone?" Rachel asked.

"People don't need to come downtown much anymore. The malls and discount stores on the other side of town draw all the trade. When development revived the economy, it forced a lot of local businesses to close. The mom-and-pop stores couldn't compete with national chains and discount houses."

Rachel thought of downtown Morgan's Point where both sides of Main Street were lined with small, thriving businesses. Perkins' Ice Cream Emporium, Wilbert's Hardware and Dottie's Kurl Up and Dye Salon had all been operating for years. Women bought their dresses at the Stylish Boutique and their groceries at Green's Market. Three generations of local children had made their Christmas wish lists based on the current inventory of the Hobby Horse Toy Shoppe. Many of the businesses had passed from one generation to the next, upholding traditions of friendly, personal service in the process.

"That used to be the busiest place in town." Joe waved a hand toward the town square. "It's empty now, but after dark, it'll come alive. I hear there's a lot of gang activity down here then."

Rachel resented this obvious object lesson of Joe's, but she couldn't help but be moved by the sad state of downtown Sinola. The middle of the square was marked only by a few rusty benches and a couple of die-hard pigeons roosting on the crusty green statue of a long-dead hero.

"My father used to bring me here on market day when I was a kid," Joe told her. "Farmers from outlying areas would park on Main Street, sell their produce and renew friendships. One of my favorite parts of the day was having lunch at the Flamingo Diner. I could sit for hours and listen to the old-timers tell their stories. The cook there made the best greasy cheeseburgers I've ever eaten. Nothing like the ones you get at the drive-through places."

Thinking of the curious little boy Joe had been, Rachel said nothing and he drove on. On the west side of town, things began to pick up. Again, the street was lined with gas stations, motels and restaurants. They seemed to do a brisk tourist trade if the number of out-of-state license plates was any indication.

"How far is it to the main highway?" Rachel asked.

"About three miles. But that's not too far to drive for true bargains." He turned into the parking lot of the Sinola Factory Outlet Mall. The immense gray structure was built for utility, not beauty. It seemed to crouch in the middle of a concrete parking lot as huge as Walt Disney World's. Rows of matching storefronts flanked the main building, giving it the imposing and inhospitable facade of a fortress.

Rachel figured the gigantic American flags waving in the breeze high above the mall served to attract business from the interstate, not to represent patriotism. On closer inspection the patches of well-manicured grass that she'd seen from the street turned out to be green-painted concrete.

"Charming," she said.

"The stores here sell discounted textiles, furniture, jewelry, clothing, pottery. And it's all factory direct. You name it and you can find it here. Of course, it'll probably be an irregular, but then quality is a highly overrated commodity these days."

"It seems like a success," she remarked. The parking lot was full.

"I guess it would to someone who's only interested in money."

"Is that what you think of me, Joe?"

He started at the sound of his name on her lips. She'd always called him Morgan or Mayor. *Joe* was nice. "You've given me no reason to think otherwise."

"Do you think I don't realize how ugly all this commercialism is?"

"Do you?"

"Yes. But I also realize that it has brought jobs and revenue into this town. Those little mom-and-pop stores didn't do that."

"Let me ask you just one thing, Rachel. Would you want to live in Sinola?"

She was silent for a long moment. "Okay, Morgan, you made your point."

"What do you mean?"

"I mean I feel like Jimmy Stewart in the movie *It's a Wonderful Life*. You know the part where Clarence the angel shows George Bailey what Bedford Falls would be like if he'd never been born? I'm sorry things didn't turn out better in Sinola, but obviously, this is a result of poor planning. Disasters like this don't have to happen."

"It's inevitable when outsiders come in and take over. Developers don't know anything about Morgan's Point. They don't know what the local people care about. They don't have to live here and they don't give a damn. The bottom line is, they want to make a profit. This is one way to do it."

"But it's not the only way."

"I'm not willing to take that chance. You'll never convince me that the risk is worth the potential for disaster."

"And you'll never convince me that Morgan's Point should be insulated from the world like a place caught in a time warp."

"Then I guess we've reached an impasse," he said quietly.

When the tour of Sinola was over, Joe turned the Jeep toward Morgan's Point, driving back the way they'd come. He'd done what he'd set out to. He'd made his point. The rest was up to Rachel. When they reached Trader's Oak, he turned off the road onto a track that was scarcely more than flattened-out grass.

"Where are we going?" she wanted to know.

"To have lunch."

"In the woods?" she asked skeptically.

"I know a great little spot. It's quiet and we can talk."

"I thought we agreed that wouldn't be a good idea." She panicked at the thought of being alone in the woods with Joe. To talk or do anything else.

"I never agreed," he said as he braked the Jeep. He jumped out and retrieved a large basket from the back. "Lunch," he said simply as he started off for Trader's Oak.

"Morgan! Is that a picnic?" Rachel climbed out of the Jeep and followed him.

"It sure is."

"That's not fair. You never said anything about any picnic."

"I guess I forgot."

"You didn't forget. You schemed this whole thing to get me alone in the woods."

He threw back his head and laughed, but kept on walking. "The only thing I schemed to do was have a sandwich. You can have one, too, if you're willing to be civil. If not, I suggest you go back to the Jeep and wait for me there."

"Maybe I'll just walk back to town," she retorted.

"Suit yourself. It's five miles as the crow flies." His long arm pointed the way. "And ninety-five degrees in the shade."

She ran until she'd closed the gap between them. Then she grabbed his arm and spun him around. "You know, Morgan, I've never said this to a man before. I always thought it was something you only heard in old movies. But now I can say it and mean it. You are totally insufferable."

"Actually, I'm hungry." He walked on.

"I never should have come here today. I don't know what possessed me to agree to spend a whole morning with you."

He stopped, dropped the basket to the ground and took her in his arms. "The same thing that has possessed me since the first time I saw you. This," he said as his mouth closed over hers.

For an instant, Rachel considered struggling to force their lips apart. But just for an instant. As he pulled her close and she felt the warmth of his hard body, she knew she would not resist. Only a fool would deny herself so much pleasure. Damn, but the man knew how to kiss.

That was her last thought for several minutes. As the kiss continued beyond the safety point, all her attention focused on the areas he was touching. Her lips, which tingled with need and desire. Her breasts, which were pressed against his broad chest. Her thighs, which were captured between his. Her energy seemed to concentrate in her blood, which raced and sang through her body. This was no ordinary kiss.

This was no ordinary man.

This was different. It was real.

After a few moments, Joe set Rachel away from him. Her eyes were still closed, her lips rosy from the work-out. "That's why you came today, Rachel. Don't kid yourself."

His deep voice brought her back from the fantasy land she'd strayed into. "Oh, Morgan. You're so romantic."

"I tried that. Remember? You rejected my flowers."

"I thought those were for my mother."

"I just said that to save face. I brought them for you, you dope. Just like I packed the picnic for you. Like I shaved for you and wore my best shirt for you."

"Really?" she asked softly.

"Yes, really. Now shut up and come and eat." He picked up the basket. Pulling out a plaid blanket, he spread it on the ground under the big oak tree and sat down on it.

Rachel stood rooted to the spot, trying to accept what she'd just heard. "You did all that for me? Why?"

He was busy pulling plastic-wrapped sandwiches out of the basket. "Because I like you."

Surely she'd misunderstood. "You like me?"

"Yeah."

"Why?"

"Damned if I know. There's certainly nothing about you to like." He motioned impatiently for her to join him. "You're as homely as a mud fence post. You're fat and lumpy and lazy and stupid. I can't imagine what I see in you."

She sat down on the blanket. "I thought I was a self-centered, money-grubbing capitalist."

"You're that, too. Do you want pimento cheese or chicken salad?"

"I'll take the cheese." She bit into her sandwich and studied Joe thoughtfully. He sure knew how to knock the pins out from under a girl. He liked her. Was that so terrible? According to her mother, he was one of the nicest young men she knew. Maybe if they could reconcile their differences, something might develop. That kiss had certainly felt like something.

"Why won't you let anyone get close to you, Rachel?"

"I'm close to lots of people."

"Like who?"

"My mother. Clay. My sister, Molly."

"Family doesn't count. Have you ever been in love?"

She didn't answer right away; she wanted to be honest. "No," she said at last. "I guess not. I've never had the time."

"I knew it."

"How could you be so sure?"

"Because you're an emotional miser. You keep your feelings locked up inside. When someone does try to reach you, you talk about chicken pox and itches and then you change the subject."

"I resent your judging me."

"Resent all you like. You're going to listen. For some reason, you're afraid to let anyone get close, to know the secret you. You're afraid of being found out, so you keep your distance. You bury yourself in work and fill up your appointment book so you won't realize how empty your life really is."

She stiffened. No one was supposed to figure that out. What made Joe Morgan so smart? "Are you finished?"

"Not yet. You don't have to be afraid of me, Rachel. I've been in love."

"Do you want a medal?"

"I've been there and I know what hell it can be if you love the wrong person."

"You do?" His astute analysis unnerved her. When had she dropped her guard? What had she said or done that gave him an inside track to her feelings?

"Do you remember what you said to me this morning?"

"Which time?"

"About the citations. That I was upset because you turned me down."

"Yes?"

"For your information, I did not tell Wayne to give you those tickets. Honest. If I'd thought of it, however, I would have. That's how frustrated you make me. It's hard on a man's ego to think he's unattractive to a woman."

"I never said that. It's because I find you so attractive that I don't want to like you."

"What does that mean?"

"It means I feel funny when you kiss me."

"Funny, like you want to burst out laughing?"

"No, dummy. Funny, like my insides are melting."

He brightened. "That's good."

"No, that's terrible. We're as different as night and day. We'll never agree on anything."

He took her sandwich out of her hand and set it aside. Then he pulled her into his lap. "We agree on the melty insides thing."

She laughed. "It's not much to base a relationship on."

"It's a start." He laid her down on the blanket, covering her body with his. One hand stroked her hair and the other slipped open the buttons of her blouse. He parted the material and caressed her breast through the silky fabric of her bra. She strained against him and pulled his mouth down on hers. There was nothing gentle about this kiss. It was full of need and demand.

He loosened her bra and she trembled when his strong fingers kneaded the tender flesh of her breast. Her blood ran hot when his mouth seared a path down her chest to capture the tender bud. He teased and caressed before giving the other equal time. Rachel stopped thinking and gave herself up to the sheer pleasure of his touch.

This was dangerous, Joe told himself. He was alone with a beautiful woman, miles from another human being. There were no ringing telephones to interrupt them, no risk of discovery. Judging from Rachel's heated response, he could carry this event to its logical conclusion.

Wasn't that what he wanted? To possess Rachel in every sense of the word? To know what it felt like to lose himself in her sweetness? If he could make her his, he might change her mind about Cypress Knoll. Maybe he could teach her to compromise.

He kissed her again, more passionately than before, in hopes of dislodging the niggling doubt that had entered his thoughts. What was wrong with him? He didn't want to make love to Rachel so he could change her mind.

No. He wanted to change her mind so that he could make love to her. There was a big difference.

With a groan, he rolled onto his back and covered his eyes with his arm. "Oh, Rachel, you're going to kill me."

She lay there, breathing heavily, wondering about what had almost just happened. She had been ready to give herself to Joe Morgan, a man she barely knew and wasn't even sure she liked. What was worse, she'd been ready to do so out in the open on a plaid blanket under a tree. What was happening to her? She didn't do things like that.

"Rachel?" Joe's voice was husky.

"What?" Her voice was a whisper.

"Button your blouse. I'm afraid of what might happen if I see your breasts again."

Rachel sat up and hastily straightened her clothing. She tried for calmness. "I think what we need to do is finish our sandwiches, drive back to town and forget this ever happened."

"I agree."

"You do?" She was sorry that he had given up so easily. Parts of her body still hummed from his touch and she secretly wanted another of those hot kisses. But she would die before she would tell him that.

"In theory." He gathered her into his arms and dropped little kisses on her face. "In practice, I'm not sure I can forget."

She pulled away and scrambled to her feet. "I'm willing to try, if you are. We both know that nothing can come of this silly attraction we feel for each other. I'm a city girl. I don't even like fresh air. Your roots go back to the beginning of this provincial little town. I like unrelenting activity—it's how I operate. You like gliding on the porch. I can't see eye to eye with a man whose idea of excitement is watching hummingbirds. It's best if we simply acknowledge the spark between us and then ignore it.''

There was a certain logic in her words, even if he didn't believe them. "Do you think you can do that? Can you ignore the way you feel when I touch you?"

She started back toward the Jeep. "There's the rub," she admitted. "I guess I'll just have to make sure that you don't touch me again."

Chapter Six

Rachel kept her promise. For the next few days, she worked at avoiding Joe and refused to take his calls. If she was going to go all melty when she was with him, she'd make damn sure she wasn't within touching distance of him.

She made a trip to Jacksonville to check on things and was dismayed to find that the main office was running just fine without her. She did tasks that any of her trusted employees could have handled and worked until she was good and tired. Maybe if she was exhausted, she could fall asleep without thinking of Joe Morgan. Dreaming about kissing him was almost as painful as kissing him.

One morning, she dropped her mother off at Dottie's Kurl Up and Dye Salon for her standing appointment. She became suspicious when Dottie called to tell her to pick up Lydia an hour later than usual. She hoped the ladies were just enjoying an interesting gabfest, but she was wrong.

Rachel's knuckles whitened on the steering wheel when she saw her mother walk out of the salon. Lydia's normally softly waved, gray-streaked hair was so short, Rachel suspected Dottie may have used dog-grooming clippers to cut away the hair around her ears and neck. The mass of spiky curls on top was longer, but appeared as if it had been styled with an eggbeater. "Scrunched" was what the magazines called it.

As if the youthful style weren't enough, now her mother's hair was a brilliant shade of strawberry blond.

"What do you think of my new 'do'?" Lydia asked as she got in the car and fastened her seat belt. She pulled down the sun visor, glanced into the mirror and tentatively patted her severely reduced hair. "That Dottie is so talented. It looks exactly like the picture in her new style book. Color and all. Isn't it amazing!"

"That's the word for it," Rachel agreed with a sigh. "Amazing." Her mother was so pleased and happy that Rachel didn't have the heart to tell her how she really felt. In truth, the haircut was cute, but much too youthful for a woman of fifty-five.

"You don't like it?" Lydia's voice quavered.

"I didn't say that. It's just going to take some getting used to. You've been gray for a long time."

"Too long, if you ask me." Lydia's tone became cheerful. "If Jane Fonda and Tina Turner can live their fifth decade in style, so can I."

On closer inspection, Rachel could see that her mother had the perfect skin tone for her new hair color, even if it was obvious that the shade could only have come from a bottle. Nature wasn't that generous with middle-aged women. She was about to say so when she changed her mind. Her mother needed her support, not her criticism.

Lydia frowned again. "I can tell, you don't like it."

"I'm just surprised," Rachel hedged. "I've never seen your hair so . . . so blond."

"Dottie swears I look ten years younger."

"That would be a conservative estimate, I'd say."

"So you do like it?"

"I'm sure I will once I get used to it."

Lydia patted her hair again. "I agree with Dottie. It definitely takes the years off."

"It does suggest youth." Rachel wondered if she looked as old as she felt at this minute. Seeing your mother through a second adolescence was a trying experience. "Mom, promise me you won't get your nose pierced without talking to me first."

Lydia looked at her in confusion. "My nose pierced? Goodness sakes, why would I want to do that?"

"Never mind." She started the engine and was about to pull out into traffic when Lydia gasped.

"What's wrong?"

"I just remembered. I forgot to refill my prescriptions."

"You can call Clay. He'll be happy to bring them by after he closes the pharmacy. It would give him a good excuse to stay for dinner."

"We won't have time, we have tryouts tonight."

"What tryouts?" Rachel asked with a frown.

"The Chamber Follies are next month and the auditions are tonight. It's a hoot. You don't want to miss it."

"Yes, I do and I will." Small-town talent shows were not her favorite form of entertainment. Especially when the mayor would be there.

Lydia sighed. "Joe said you wouldn't come."

Rachel's mouth went dry at the mention of his name. A tingling sensation raced down her back. "When did he say that?"

"This morning."

"You talked to Joe Morgan this morning?" she asked suspiciously.

"He just happened to drop by."

"What was he doing at the Kurl and Dye?"

"I don't remember. He complimented me on my new look and asked if I was coming to the auditions. When I told him we wouldn't miss it, he was doubtful that you'd show up. I can't recall exactly what he said."

"Never mind. At any rate, he's right. I'm not going." Steering clear of the mayor for the remainder of her stay in Morgan's Point meant staying away from civic functions. "If you'll give me your medicine bottles, I'll run into the drugstore and get them refilled."

Lydia unhooked her seat belt and opened her door. "I'll come with you and we'll have a sandwich at the fountain. I just love Hattie's chicken salad sandwiches. It's way past lunchtime, isn't it?"

"It's only a little after twelve, Mom."

Lydia hastened her step. "That late? No wonder I'm starved."

Once inside, she handed Rachel the bottles. "You drop these off and I'll turn in our order and save you a seat. It gets crowded in here at lunchtime."

Rachel chatted with Clay until she noticed the customers lining up behind her. She went to the soda fountain to look for her mother. The drugstore was a popular spot and every booth was occupied. She began to wonder if Lydia had changed her mind about eating.

Finally, she spotted the unfamiliar reddish blond head. Seated in a booth across from Joe Morgan.

"Hello, Rachel. This is a surprise," Joe said. Lydia had been alone when she'd come out of Dottie's this morning and flagged him down. She'd suggested he join her for lunch, but she hadn't said a word about Rachel. He never would have agreed if he'd known she would be here. A man could stand only so much rejection.

But she was here, so he'd have to make the most of it. He stood and motioned for her to slide into the booth. "I'll go to the counter and order another sandwich."

Rachel sat down on the outer edge of the vinyl-covered bench and when Joe returned, she allowed him to stand there, waiting. He could wait until hell froze over for all she cared.

Lydia flapped her hand. "Scoot over, dear, so Joe can sit down."

She looked up at Joe and gave him a thin smile. "Why don't you share the other seat with Mom? She's so tiny, she hardly takes up any room at all."

Joe fought the impulse to turn around and walk out, but he didn't want to give her the satisfaction. "My dry cleaning is in the way."

Lydia frowned at her daughter. "Joe was here first, dear. So scoot."

Rachel, aware of the attention they were attracting, finally scooted. She was going to have a talk with her mother. This whole thing smacked of conspiracy.

Joe slid in beside her. When his leg touched hers, he felt the sudden jolt of arousal he always experienced when she was near. "Thank you."

She jerked her leg away from his. Why did her body betray her when it came within an inch of this man? "Don't mention it."

Joe cleared his throat and did what lawyers and politicians usually did in a tight spot. He talked. "Lydia tells me she's got a new song-and-dance cooked up for the Follies."

"A dance?" Rachel exclaimed.

"I've done it every year since I moved here," Lydia replied. "Why should this year be any different?"

"Because of your injuries," Rachel pointed out logically. "You walk with a cane, Mother."

Lydia's smile was secretive and smug. "I acknowledge certain limitations, but I've got that all worked out. Besides, my physical therapist said I should stop depending on the cane so much."

"Rachel, I haven't seen much of you lately," Hattie Benson remarked as she distributed their food. She'd worked for Mr. Threadwell, and now she worked for Clay, running the fountain while he ran the pharmacy. "I need to talk to you about finding a couple of acres for my oldest boy. Ray and his wife are tired of the city and want to move back here. They'd like to build a place outside of town."

"We have several listings that might fit their needs." Rachel rolled her eyes toward Joe. "But I'd need to talk to them because there are some strict zoning requirements."

Hattie nodded. "I'd better get back to work before the boss catches me goofing off."

"If Clay says anything to you, just tell him to see me," Lydia joked.

"I'll do that, Lydia. See you tonight at the audition." She said over her shoulder to Rachel, "Maybe we can discuss those properties."

Rachel's mouth was full of chicken salad, so she nodded enthusiastically. She wasn't going to the tryouts, but she would give Hattie a call tomorrow.

"Are you and the town elders going to do your act again this year, Joe?" Lydia asked.

"No," he said with an embarrassed chuckle. "The all-male chorus line has retired. I think we all ripped our dresses in the finale last time. I volunteered to be stage manager this year."

"They were so funny, Rachel. You should have seen them. Miss Watkins, the home ec teacher, made their costumes out of bright red satin. Short dresses with feathers around the neck. They wore wigs, black hose and heels, and Dottie made up their faces. Their rendition of "Hard Hearted Hannah" brought the house down."

"Too bad I missed it." This time last year, Rachel had been working on one of the biggest deals of her career. Her mother had invited her to the Follies, but she hadn't been able to get away from the office. Or maybe she hadn't been willing to take the time off. Her hard work had paid off; she'd made a lot of money on that deal.

Now she found herself wishing she could be a small part of the fun. She felt suddenly left out, like the only person not invited to the prom.

"The sight of those guys all dolled up made a lasting impression on this town," Lydia put in. "I heard that the bulk of this year's early ticket sales were due to tales about that act. Are you sure we can't talk you into doing it again?"

Joe shook his head. No way, he thought. It had been fun, but embarrassing. He wouldn't mind leaving a lasting impression on Rachel, but he'd be damned if he would do it in a dress. "It wouldn't be as funny the second time around."

"Maybe you could do a different song?" Lydia suggested.

"I don't think so. Earl Potts had to go on a low-fat diet because of his heart attack and lost too much weight to wear his outfit. Earl's heart attack scared the Dudley twins so bad, they quit smoking and gained too much to wear theirs.''

Lydia giggled. "And I heard that Oscar's wife threatened to divorce him if he ever put on another dress. Dottie says that's because he looked better in one than she does."

"Oscar used gout as his excuse at the meeting."

The two of them laughed, but because Rachel didn't know the men in question, it wasn't as amusing to her.

"Are you doing a Rodgers and Hammerstein number again this year?" Joe asked Lydia.

The older woman's smile was full of mischief. "Nope."

"You always do something by Rodgers and Hammerstein," Rachel said. "What are you going to do?"

Lydia cocked her head to one side and shook her finger at her daughter. "That's a secret. You'll just have to wait until tonight and see."

"But I won't be there," she insisted.

"Everybody and their pet duck will be there," Lydia argued.

Rachel laughed. "Everybody except me."

Lydia sighed dramatically.

"You aren't going to bring yours, are you, Mrs. Fox?" Joe asked.

Lydia frowned, perplexed. "My what?"

"Your pet duck."

"Lord, no," Lydia exclaimed. "It would be much too crowded and noisy in the auditorium for Mrs. Puddleduck. Whatever gave you such an idea, Joe?"

He looked at Rachel, but it was obvious she wasn't going to help him out of this one. "Just thought I'd ask."

"You said I couldn't take Mrs. Puddleduck to town," Lydia said in a hurt tone. "I gave my word I wouldn't."

Joe had never had so much trouble trying to stay on the good side of women in his life. Somehow he'd managed to hurt Lydia's feelings. "I'm sorry." He leaned across the table and covered the older woman's hand with his. "I shouldn't have asked. Am I forgiven?"

Rachel found herself wishing Joe had looked at her that way, had taken her hand in his and had said those words to her after their stone-silent ride back into town last Saturday. But he hadn't said a word. When he'd dropped her off at home, he'd told her that he was willing to give her another chance and if she changed her mind about seeing him again, all she had to do was say so.

She wasn't surprised when Lydia smiled and said, "Oh, Joe, you're such a sweetie. Of course I forgive you."

"Oh, brother!" Rachel rolled her eyes. "I may go into sugar shock."

Joe turned the force of his brown-eyed gaze on her. What was the matter with her? He thought women enjoyed hearing a man apologize for something he didn't do. After what had almost happened between them last Saturday, it was hard to sit here and make polite small talk.

God, the woman scared the hell out of him. She'd been on his mind all week, but when he'd broken down and called her, she had refused to talk to him. She had told him that day that she planned to ignore him, and in doing so, she'd let him know loud and clear where he stood.

Joe glanced at his watch and slid out of the booth. "I need to get back to the office for a one o'clock appointment. I hate to eat and run, ladies, but you know how it is."

Rachel grinned. "Too bad. I hope it wasn't anything I said."

"Not at all." Joe didn't like the look of her smug victory grin. She may have won the fight but the war wasn't over yet. "A few minor cuts and abrasions, but don't worry, Rachel. As my grandpa used to say, 'They'll get well before I marry.'"

Her grin faded. Was he merely repeating an old saying or was he really planning to marry soon? She hadn't thought of that before. There were probably any number of women who would snatch him up if they could. She just didn't happen to be one of them.

So why did she suddenly feel so...worried?

"Sit down, Joe, and finish your lunch," Lydia suggested. "I promise to make Rachel behave."

"Can't." He shook his head. "Too much to do today. But I enjoyed the company."

Perversely, Rachel wanted him to stay. What was wrong with her lately? Last week she'd longed for Joe, a man she didn't like, to kiss her, and then she'd damned him for doing so. Today she'd been angry because she'd been forced to have lunch with him, and now she was saddened that she'd driven him away. She was losing it, all right. Probably too much fresh air.

"My treat," she said, snatching up the check when Joe reached for it.

Joe stiffened. No woman had ever paid his way, and he wasn't about to start with Rachel. When he tried to wrest it from her grip, the top part of the green ticket tore away.

Knowing that she was no match for him when it came to brute strength, Rachel quickly tucked the remainder into her blouse and pressed her hand over it.

He stared at her chest, recalling the passion he'd experienced when he'd touched her there, remembering the warm feel of her lips against his. His hand was in the air, reaching toward her when dishes crashed to the floor behind the counter, reminding him they were not alone this time.

He stared at her and his voice sounded harsh when he said, "Come on, Rachel, give it to me."

She recognized that hungry look in his eyes; she'd seen it before. She knew he wasn't talking about the check. Neither was she when she shook her head vehemently. "I can't."

Joe sighed. "You'll be sorry if you don't."

"It's only a lunch tab," she said to remind herself what they were arguing about.

"Stop squabbling, children," Lydia remarked. "Joe, you can pay next time."

There wouldn't be a next time, but Rachel couldn't speak when she saw the determination in his brown eyes intensify.

"I'm a patient man. I can wait." He turned to Lydia. "See you tonight."

"You bet." The older woman fumbled in her purse for her compact. When Joe was out of earshot, she gave Rachel a sour look. "Rachel, I'd be ashamed."

"For what?"

Lydia dabbed powder on her nose. "For teasing poor Joe like that when anyone can plainly see that he's smitten with you."

"I didn't tease him," she denied hotly. "And he is not smitten." Such an old-fashioned word didn't begin to describe the powerful desire that had radiated from Joe during their plaid blanket encounter.

"Of course he is, and you did." She pulled out her lipstick and took off the cap. "I call it teasing when a woman takes something a man wants and sticks it in her bosom. And I call a man smitten when he almost dives in after it, right in front of God and everybody."

Rachel plucked the check from its resting place. "I didn't do it to tease him. Anyway, the only reason he was ready to dive in after it, as you so crudely put it, was because he's a male chauvinist pig. Which is just one of his many shortcomings."

Lydia sighed. "There's something endearing about a man with old-fashioned ideas. For one thing, he respects women."

"Yes," Rachel scoffed. "As long as she stays in her place—the kitchen or the bedroom. Just let her into the boardroom and see how respectful he is."

"Joe isn't like that," Lydia denied. "You're just upset because he persuaded the town council not to sell out to that conglomerate."

"What the people around here don't seem to understand is that they can't stop progress."

"We intend to try. The people don't want to see Cypress Knoll turned into an amusement park, a shopping mall or anything else. And neither do I. We'll fight you, Rachel."

"Mother!"

"Don't look so surprised, dear. I moved here to get away from the influences of the city. Do you think I'm going to sit still and watch progress invade us like a plague?"

"Mom, you're in the business. You know that development can be good for an area."

"Some areas, maybe. But not Morgan's Point. The people here like things the way they are. This is a nice, quiet, peaceful town and that's how we want it to stay. We know and trust each other. We can't say the same for outsiders."

Rachel was silent as she considered her mother's words. After a moment, she said, "I'm an outsider. And so were you five years ago."

"I'm accepted here now. When I was in the hospital, I found out how many friends I have. You saw all the cards and flowers I got. With Molly off in Montana and you always so busy in Jacksonville, the people in this town have been like family to me."

"I haven't been a very good daughter, have I?"

Lydia reached across the table and clasped Rachel's hands in hers. "You've been a wonderful daughter. That's why I love you. I want you to be happy, but you need to learn there's more to life than work."

"My work has always been important to me."

"Honey, it's not the work you crave. It's security. You're like a little squirrel, running around crazy, storing up far more nuts than you'll ever be able to eat. Just so you won't have to depend on anyone else. Needing someone isn't necessarily bad."

"It's not necessarily good, either."

Lydia put away her cosmetics. "You've been here a few weeks now. Tell me how you feel about this town."

"As you said, it's a nice, tidy, little place. It's only minutes off the beaten path. Extremely low crime rate. Very little unemployment, good schools."

Her mother shook her head. "I don't want you to sell it to me, I want to know how you *feel* about it. The other day when you went to Jacksonville, how did you feel when you turned off the Interstate toward home at the end of the day?"

Rachel recalled that she'd been exhausted after a long day of property tours, hours of working on contracts and looking for an elusive error in the escrow account. She had been surprised and a little disappointed that the business seemed to be thriving without her daily input. Then she'd felt frustrated because she had to drive back to Morgan's Point, instead of going home and crashing in her own bed.

But when she'd taken the Morgan's Point exit and left the traffic on the highway, an overwhelming sense of tranquillity had settled over her. By the time she pulled into the driveway, all the tensions of the day had faded.

"Well," Lydia prodded.

"I was glad to get out of all that traffic, and I was tired."

"What were you thinking?"

Rachel refused to admit that her thoughts had included Joe. "I was thinking how attractive the town is and how much potential it has. When I was in the city, I heard that the Margolian brothers are looking for an outlet mall site. I wrote them a letter about Morgan's Point."

"Oh, Rachel, is there any hope for you?" Lydia sighed. "Maybe Joe's right. It all comes down to money, doesn't it?"

"I want the same things other women want, Mom. I really do. I want a man to love and I want to be loved by him in return. I want to have children someday, too. But I want to be responsible for my own happiness. What's wrong with that?"

"Nothing. Unless it keeps you from loving someone."

"Regardless of what Joe Morgan thinks, money is not the driving force in my life. But it is important to me, and it has been ever since I learned that without it, you're nothing."

"I understand why you feel the way you do, but you could live off the interest from your investment income for the rest of your life. You could even support a family."

Rachel hoped a little humor would deflect her mother's uncomfortable questions. She grinned and asked, "Are you saying it's time for the artificial babies?"

"No, I'm saying it's high time you started thinking about the rest of your life and what you plan to do with it. I don't want any artificial stuff for you. I want you to experience the real thing."

Chapter Seven

Rachel refused to attend the tryouts. Since her encounter with Joe in the drugstore, she was even more determined to avoid him. Her visit to Sinola had proved that she could learn to like him, and his quiet little town, too much. When she dropped her mother off at the door of the high school auditorium, she asked, "What time shall I pick you up?"

"There's no need for that, dear. Ernie will bring me home. Are you sure you won't come in and watch for a while?"

"I'd rather not, Mom. I need to get home."

"And do what, pray tell? There's not a single thing in this world that can't wait until tomorrow."

"There are certain people whose paths I would rather not cross at this time, if you don't mind."

"Rachel, Rachel. Why don't you give poor Joe a chance?"

"That's exactly what I am not going to do," she said firmly.

Lydia got out of the car. "You are hopeless. Go home, then."

Rachel watched her walk into the building and thought her mother's step had a little more spring in it than before. She was pleased by the older woman's new confidence; she would soon discard the cane and be completely independent. If you didn't count the goofy hairdo, Lydia was behaving more responsibly lately. Maybe she was learning to accept and cope with her impairments. Rachel smiled wryly. Lydia's impairments didn't seem to affect her insight into her daughter's behavior.

There had been a time when Rachel had doubted it, but now she was sure that her mother would eventually be able to live alone again. When that time came, and it wasn't far away, Rachel could return to Jacksonville, to her own home, to her work and to her life. She reminded herself that she wasn't cut out to live in a place like Morgan's Point. Charming it may be, but she didn't belong here.

As she drove down the empty street, lined with tall pines, she felt a restlessness creep over her. She decided to stop for a double dip of pistachio almond ice cream. That would make her feel better. As she drove by Perkins', she noticed that the ice-cream parlor was closed. Everything was closed, she realized as she scanned the darkened storefronts. Everyone was either at the auditorium or at home taking care of their families.

She drove toward her mother's house at well over the twenty-five-mile-per-hour speed limit. No red lights flashing in her rearview mirror meant that even Officer Hacker had a talent to audition.

As she opened the front door, she remembered that she hadn't locked her car. It didn't matter, even with half the police force at the tryouts, there was no need to lock up. The criminal element hadn't yet discovered Morgan's Point. Obviously, Joe Morgan was determined to keep it that way.

Rachel plopped down on the sofa and picked up the television remote control. She flipped through the channels, but nothing caught her interest and she quickly flicked off the set. She was definitely restless. Not just a little bit. A lot. There was no paperwork to do, nothing to kill time. Boredom like this was what drove sane women to take up needlepoint.

"If I was in Jacksonville right now," she grumbled to the silent room, "there would be plenty of alternatives to sitting home in an empty house." There was the theater, and a choice of movies every night, not just on the weekend. Cozy little bars, big nightclubs with entertainment. When she wasn't in the mood for any of those, there had always been a bulging briefcase to keep her occupied.

She lay down, propped her head on a sofa pillow and tried to brood about all the things she missed by being here, but the reality of her life kept intruding. Face it, kid, she told herself, even in Jacksonville, you'd be sitting home alone. Unless she was entertaining clients, and sometimes that could be tedious, she rarely went out.

At home, she would at least have the option of calling a friend. But whom? She'd never taken the time to cultivate close relationships. What was it that Joe had called her that day at Trader's Oak? An emotional miser. Someone who couldn't let people get close. He'd been right; the name was appropriate. If it was true that women got to know each other by sharing things about themselves, it was no surprise that she had no good women friends. She'd never been able to do that. It wasn't that she had any deep, dark secrets. She'd never done anything she needed to hide. She simply felt her thoughts and feelings were her own business.

Nobody got all bent out of shape when men kept to themselves. But let a woman try to be the strong, silent type, and the world came unglued.

Work was her answer to the nagging loneliness she sometimes felt. Most days, she stayed at the office until early evening, then went home and returned the phone calls she hadn't had time for during the day. In Jacksonville, there were no empty hours in which to feel restless and unfulfilled. She was busy instead. Her life had seemed full.

She sat up, relieved that she'd discovered something. She wasn't lonely at all; she was bored. She needed a project to take her mind off herself. She needed the Margolian brothers. She went to the phone and dialed their office number even though it was after 7:00 p.m. If no one answered, she'd just call again in the morning.

"Dan Margolian, here," a husky male voice answered curtly.

She wasn't surprised when the developer answered his own phone. When working late, she always took calls, too. The bigger the business, the more you hated to risk missing something important. It could cost you.

"Mr. Margolian, this is Rachel Fox. We met a few months ago at Toni Benwalter's housewarming."

"Ah, yes," he replied vaguely.

"I sold Toni the new house," she reminded him.

"I remember. You're the sexy brunette who owns her own real-estate company. Did you send me a letter recently?" She heard the sound of papers being rustled.

Rachel ground her teeth at his sexist comment. Men couldn't understand why women hated such remarks because they would only be flattered if a woman said, "Oh, you're the hairy brute who owns his own company." She'd forgotten how obnoxious Margolian could be, but then business was business. She didn't have to like the man to take his money.

"I own Fox Realty and, yes, I sent you a letter about possibly locating one of your outlet mall ventures near Morgan's Point. I understand you and your brother plan to build outside of Jacksonville soon."

"Yes, but to be perfectly honest with you, Rachel, I was hoping to locate on the other side of the city. Marketing surveys indicate more consumer growth in that area."

"So, you've already chosen a site?"

"Nothing definite yet, but Rob and I will be making our decision soon."

She breathed a sigh of relief. That meant they'd found a site, but there was some kind of snag. Maybe they couldn't agree on a price. She still had a chance to convince them.

"I was hoping to entice you and your brother into taking a look at some choice property here, but if your mind is made up..." She let her words trail away.

There was an instant of silence before he said, "We'll need at least eight hundred acres."

"No problem," she replied quickly, knowing that it was a big problem. "Sounds as if this mall is going to be something else."

Dan Margolian chuckled. "It is, but we have one or two more things in mind for future expansion."

"Which you don't care to elaborate on at this time," she guessed.

"You're sharp, Rachel. I wouldn't mind doing business with you. I guess it won't hurt to take a look at this proposed site of yours." There was a slight pause and Rachel suspected he was looking at his calendar. "I have a few hours free on Thursday evening, the twenty-third. Is that a good time for you?"

He was booked solid for the next three weeks? Rachel sighed enviously. She'd once kept that kind of pace herself, and it hadn't been all that long ago. These days, she didn't need to consult her appointment book, but she waited several heartbeats before she answered. "That works for me. What time should I expect you?"

"About 6:00 p.m. I'll pick you up at your office and we'll drive down together."

Rachel explained briefly why that wouldn't be necessary.

"I'm sorry to hear about your mother," he sympathized. "I'll pick you up between six-thirty and seven in Morgan's Point and you can give me the grand tour."

Rachel relayed directions to her mother's house and hung up the phone. Still smiling, she stood up and danced around the couch. "Yes, yes, yes," she exclaimed. "That's just what I need. A project to keep my mind busy." And her body too tired to long for Joe Morgan.

Filled with a sense of purpose, she dug into the files that she'd brought to the house from the Morgan's Point office and pulled every listing she could find. Even if she could have lumped them together, they wouldn't add up to eight hundred acres. Cypress Knoll was the only answer.

She'd have to go to the town council again, but this time she'd plan her strategy better. She had three weeks to cajole and convince the townspeople that a big new mall would do them more good than a nasty old wildlife habitat. Okay, so nobody had liked the idea of an amusement park, but what harm could a few outlet stores on the outskirts of town do? Not only that, but there was the added incentive of over a million dollars in the city's treasury even after her percentage.

That fact should win a lot of votes. They could enlarge the school, build a theater, make whatever municipal improvements were necessary. They could build a clinic. Who wouldn't want that?

Joe Morgan, that was who. He would be her biggest obstacle. Rachel had battled him before and lost. But this time would be different. She knew him now and she would be prepared for whatever opposition he set in her path.

She felt a little pang of guilt but quickly quelled it. She really didn't want to choose sides against Joe, but he'd already shown that he wasn't open to compromise. If only he didn't make her feel all the emotions she didn't want to feel. Every time he touched her, she yearned for the very things that threatened her independence.

Before she'd met him, her idea of the perfect life had been marriage to a faceless, but prominent man. A man who was too busy with his own life to intrude on hers. A man to accompany her to the opera and other social events. Not that she was so crazy about the opera or ballet, but both were wonderful places to make contacts.

Now, when she had daydreams, it was always Joe Morgan at her side, touching her, driving her mad with desire. Not only had he invaded her innermost thoughts, but several children with soft brown eyes often tagged along, snuggling in her lap, clinging to her legs. What was wrong with her? She'd rarely thought about children before Joe, other than to assume she would probably have one. Someday.

She had to do something to get him out of her head. Normally, completely and diametrically opposed viewpoints would have been enough, but it was different with Joe. It was hard to deny the frightening chemistry between them, but if it could be done, she was just the woman to do it.

She was so keyed up, she couldn't sit still. She decided to go for a drive but eventually ended up at the auditorium. She sat in the parking lot for fifteen minutes and when no one came out, she went in to see if the tryouts were over. Once inside the high school, it was easy to slip unnoticed into the darkened hall and take a seat in the back row. The only lights were the ones illuminating the stage.

Her mother had talked about the Follies for years and invited Rachel many times, but she'd always been too busy to attend. Now she wished she hadn't been so quick to turn down those invitations. The people of Morgan's Point really knew how to put on a show. What they lacked in talent, they made up for in enthusiasm. They worked together with a real spirit of cooperation, sharing a common goal.

That kind of camaraderie and fellowship was special and Rachel wondered if she would ever experience it. Morgan's Point had embraced her mother, an outsider. But would acceptance come as easily for her if she defeated the mayor and brought the reality of the outside world to the town's doorstep?

She watched several acts and had to sit on her hands to keep from applauding, lest she draw attention to herself. Then Lydia vamped onto the stage to the beat of the offbeat rock song, "I'm Too Sexy." At first, Rachel was appalled by her mother's choice of material, but she had a good voice and a natural rhythm. She played it up with comedic effect and her campy antics made it clear that she was not taking herself seriously. Rachel was soon as caught up in the performance as those in the front rows.

By the time Lydia hit the last note, everyone was cheering and shouting that she would be the hit of the show. Rachel didn't doubt it. She grudingly admitted that her mom was talented and had the newfound nerve to use it. It had taken a brain injury to give Lydia the courage, or maybe it was the disinhibition, to "go for it" as Clay would say. Would Rachel ever figure out what she wanted? Better yet, if she did, would she have the guts to go for it?

She decided to slip out as quietly as she'd slipped in. When she stood up to leave, she found Joe blocking the aisle.

"Your mother's act is great," he said. "Did you sneak in here because you were worried she would embarrass you?"

"I wasn't sneaking. I was being quiet so I wouldn't disturb anyone. I just wanted to make sure she wasn't going to try to tap dance or something. How did you know I was here?"

"Someone saw you pull into the parking lot."

"The mayor has spies everywhere."

"Just interested parties. Can we talk?"

"About what?" she demanded.

He took a deep breath and looked intently into her eyes. Grasping her arm, he led her to a dark corner outside the auditorium. He relinquished his hold on her and said softly, "About you and me. About what's happening between us."

"I don't want to talk about that."

"This is one time I don't care what you want."

He took a step forward and Rachel felt an irresistible urge to walk into his arms. But good sense prevailed and she backed up. It wouldn't be long before he found out about her call to Dan Margolian. When he did, he would leave her alone. He'd probably never speak to her again.

Now why did that bother her enough to bring a tear to her eye? It was what she'd wanted all along. Before he could notice, she brushed past him and marched down the hall. She was angry with herself for such a blatant display of emotion. And mad at Joe for causing it.

He caught up with her in the parking lot. He gently grabbed her arm and turned her to face him. "I don't know why I keep trying."

"Neither do I, but I wish you'd learn to take no for an answer." Her throat was thick with tears. She never cried, especially over men. Leave it to Joe to bring out the worst in her.

"I'm kind of stubborn that way."

"Nothing can come of it, so please just go away."

Joe grinned. "But *something* could and that's the problem."

Once again, Rachel called anger to her rescue. She shrugged off his grasp. "I don't want to have an affair with you." That much was true. She wanted much more than that.

"I don't want that, either."

"So what do you want?"

"I want you, Rachel. Enough that I'm willing to cut a deal."

"I don't want to deal with you."

"Okay then, a compromise." He reached out for her, but she sidestepped.

"Your virtue or mine?" she retorted.

"A professional compromise. Are you interested?"

She frowned. "I'm listening."

Joe breathed a sigh of relief. "I learned recently about a letter you wrote to a large development company."

Rachel threw up her hands. "I don't believe it! My own mother ratted on me."

"Lydia never mentioned it," he said quickly.

"But nobody else knew about it. I typed it and mailed it myself." Realization dawned and she glared at him. "Is the postmaster on your payroll?"

"No, but he's a concerned citizen. He didn't say which company and I didn't ask."

"Isn't there a law against such things? I could get him fired."

"He felt so guilty, he put in for his retirement the same day he told me."

"Did he also tell you what the letter was about?" she countered.

"He didn't open it. He just said it was pretty hefty."

"What's this all about? And where does the compromise fit in?"

"I know you're up to something, and I can only surmise that it involves Cypress Knoll." He paused, giving her the opportunity to make up a story that would throw him off the track.

She stared into his eyes. She refused to lie to him, but she had no intention of confessing, either. "I won't discuss my business plans with you."

"I was right about you." He smiled. "You're an honest woman and I believe I can trust you. That's very important to me."

"Get to the point, Mayor."

He took a deep breath and plunged ahead with the harebrained scheme he'd dreamed up. "I want us to spend some quality time together, get to know each other better. If you will agree to that, then I promise not to go on an all-out campaign against you with the townspeople."

Rachel laughed derisively. "I can't believe you think I'd be foolish enough to fall for that. I've never doled out sexual favors to make a sale and I don't intend to start with you."

"I'm not asking for sexual favors," he said defensively. "I just want a chance to show you that, even though we're on opposite sides, we can still have a relationship. I think the attraction we feel for each other is strong enough to overcome our differences."

"And in exchange for that measly chance you're willing to sell out the people of Morgan's Point? I don't believe you."

"I'm not willing to go that far," he admitted. "I still want to see that land turned into a sanctuary for wildlife, but I promise not to use any dirty tactics against you. You have my word on it."

During their last fracas over Cypress Knoll, Joe hadn't used the underhanded tricks she'd been prepared for. As much as it galled her to admit, he was above all that. "You wouldn't know a dirty tactic if it walked up and bit you on the behind."

"You don't know me very well. I'm basically honest, but I can be ruthless when it comes to fighting for something I care about. I care about Morgan's Point and I hope to preserve Cypress Knoll for future generations. If it comes to a showdown, I'll fight for what I want, but I'll fight fair."

Rachel believed him, but trust wasn't something she gave lightly. "I never doubted it for a moment. And if, as you say, it comes to a showdown, I'm sure you would use any means at your disposal."

"Not against you. I promise that when the time comes, I'll simply state my case and give my honest opinion. We'll let the people decide and may the best man win."

Rachel put him to the test. "I won't go to bed with you, and if you start pressuring me, the deal's off."

Joe grinned and raised his right hand. "I swear not to take advantage of you, even if you beg me to do so."

"Pompous ass," she muttered as she got into her car. Why was she even considering his ridiculous offer? Maybe because it would give her a chance to get her way and not be a total outcast. She'd come to admire the people of Morgan's Point and their acceptance was important to her. She gave herself a mental kick for only thinking of herself.

Joe stuffed his hands in his pockets and watched her rev the sleek car's engine. He was filled with new hope and longed to call her back. He managed to restrain himself.

The automatic window slid down noiselessly. "So, when do we start this . . . this . . ."

"Courtship?" His grin was cocky, but it was just as devastating as ever.

"Compromise," she insisted.

"How about having dinner with me tomorrow night?"

"Tomorrow night! That's too soon."

"There's no point delaying the inevitable, Rachel. Besides, I plan to show you that living in Morgan's Point has some very distinct advantages."

"You've got your work cut out for you. I'm a city girl."

"If I thought that was true, I'd have given up a long time ago." Joe had thought about it a lot lately; in fact he'd thought of little else. "What you are, is a country girl who doesn't know it yet. Why, I'll have you running barefoot in the grass before this is all over."

Rachel shivered despite the heat of the humid evening. Barefoot? What came next? Pregnant? "No way, wise guy."

"We'll see. Is seven o'clock good for you?"

"Great," she mumbled, "Just great."

"Try to show a little more enthusiasm, Rachel. I promise this is going to be painless."

Oh, there would be pain all right. Hers. Overwhelmed by her own emotions, Rachel was letting Joe Morgan's charm get to her. He was so persuasive, he had almost convinced her that things could work out for them. That in his capable hands, their puny problems didn't stand a chance.

Heaven help her, she wanted to believe him.

Chapter Eight

Joe had been on Rachel's mind when she went to sleep last night and thoughts of their coming date had plagued her most of the day. She could hardly concentrate for worrying about what he really expected from her. He'd promised not to try and get her into bed and she wasn't sure if she found that fact reassuring or dismaying. He'd called their arrangement a courtship, but she wasn't inclined to be that generous. Even so, courtships were meant to progress slowly and if he so much as kissed her tonight, the deal was off.

It was a bad idea anyway. Whoever heard of having a friendly relationship with an enemy? She no longer wanted Joe to be her enemy, but with Cypress Knoll between them, how could it be otherwise?

"Rachel." Lydia's voice interrupted her thoughts. "Would you check Mrs. Puddleduck's water before you leave? I'd do it myself, but Ernie's in a hurry." The older couple were on their way to the drugstore for a quick sandwich; then it was on to the senior citizen's hall for a rousing game of bingo. Now that Lydia's clothes and youthful hairstyle reflected her new outlook on life, she seemed content to occasionally attend "old folk" functions.

"I'll take care of it." Rachel hadn't ventured into the backyard in several days. She and Mrs. Puddleduck seemed to have an unspoken agreement; Rachel didn't infringe on her territory and she didn't infringe on Rachel's.

It was one minute before seven when she stepped outside on the back patio. She'd timed things carefully. With any luck at all, the punctual mayor would knock on the front door and when she didn't answer, he'd think he'd been stood up. Then he'd go away and she wouldn't have to do this.

Normally, when Rachel ventured into the backyard alone, Mrs. Puddleduck greeted her appearance with an obnoxious quacking guaranteed to wake the dead. This time, not only was the crazy duck not quacking, she was nowhere about. Rachel checked her favorite nesting places, but could not locate the bird. At last she bent over and, carefully keeping her distance lest she get her nose pinched, peeked into the doghouse that had been converted into a duck shelter.

"There you are, you little dictator." At first glance, Rachel thought the animal was asleep, but Mrs. Puddleduck's eyes were open and her halfhearted quack of protest at Rachel's intrusion sounded hoarse.

"It won't do you any good to try to hide in that doghouse. I'll just come in and get you," said a male voice behind her.

At the sound of Joe's voice, Rachel's head jerked up and banged against the roof of the little structure.

"Ouch!" She rubbed her head, mindless of the mess she made of her hair. "I wasn't trying to hide. Mrs. Puddleduck's in there and she won't come out."

"What did you do to her?"

Rachel glared at him. "Nothing. I came out to check her water bowl and when the old biddy didn't attack me, I thought she might have died, or at the very least, run away."

He grinned the grin that always made her want to kiss it right off his face. "No such luck, huh?"

"I admit she's not a favorite of mine, but I don't want anything to happen to her."

Joe patted Rachel on the back. "You might act tough, but I knew all along that you had a heart hidden in there somewhere."

"For Mother's sake," she added quickly.

"We have a date, remember? Go brush your hair and let's go. You've stalled long enough." Joe took her hand and would have pulled her to her feet, but the look on her face made him release her. "What's wrong?"

"Puddleduck didn't try to bite me and she didn't ruffle her feathers the way she usually does when she sees me."

"Maybe she's learned to accept you. Look how long it took you to stop flapping whenever I come around."

"She sounds weird when she quacks. She's just lying in there, looking pitiful." Rachel's eyes narrowed. "Could someone have poisoned her?"

He carefully reached inside the doghouse, gently scooped up the duck and brought her outside for a closer look. "She does seem a little droopy, but don't go jumping to conclusions. I can't think of one person in this town who would do such a thing."

"Bertie Caldwell is a jealous woman, and jealous women are capable of cruelty."

"Bertie might have been jealous of Lydia and Ernie at first, but she's found herself a truck driver over in Sinola. She's annoying at times, but she's not cruel." Joe raised the bird's head and stared into its lackluster eyes. The animal gave no protest and lay listlessly in his arms. "Maybe she just has a cold."

"A cold! In August?" Rachel shook her head. "That duck is in serious condition. She's probably been poisoned. Poor Mother."

Cradling Mrs. Puddleduck with one arm, Joe took Rachel's arm and pulled her to her feet. "She'll be all right. We just need to get her to the vet."

"Right," she agreed, casually taking her hand from his as she smoothed her rumpled skirt. She'd chosen the navy-and-rose print skirt and matching blouse because Joe had advised her not to dress up. However, he hadn't taken his own advice. His dark suit and crisp shirt and tie was about as dressed up as she had ever seen him.

"But it's after seven," she said. "Surely all the vet offices are closed by now."

"We only have only two and they're both good friends of mine. Even if they weren't, Bill and Madison would never turn away a sick animal just because it's after hours." Joe held out his hand. "Come on. Let's go."

The feeling of letting someone else take charge wasn't half bad, Rachel thought. In fact, it felt pretty good to allow another to make decisions. She took the hand he offered, and said, "Let's hurry."

It was a fifteen-minute drive to the Taylor home outside of town. The young married couple were both veterinarians and operated the only animal hospital in the area.

Puddleduck lay in Rachel's lap, unprotesting and quiet. It was true that Rachel had often envisioned the bird à l'orange, but now that it might actually die, she felt rather badly about her ill wishes.

"Hi, Madison," Joe said when a young dark-haired, bright-eyed woman with an equally bright-eyed toddler astride her hip opened the door. He introduced the two young women. "As you can see, we have a problem."

Dr. Taylor stepped aside. "Please, come in."

A young man, feeding a bottle to the baby on his lap, stood up and Joe introduced him as Dr. Bill Taylor. "I'd ask what brings you out this way, but I can see you've got a pretty sick bird on your hands."

Madison set the youngster on his feet and said, "Davey, show Joe your animals, while Mommy takes care of the sick duck."

Davey toddled across the room to a corner filled with toys. He picked up a stuffed cat and held it up for Joe's inspection. "Tat."

Joe turned Mrs. Puddleduck over to Madison's care and bent down on one knee. "Yes, Davey, that's a cat. When did you learn to talk, big guy?" He glanced at the boy's father. "Last time I was here he was still jabbering."

Bill laughed. "That's still his primary form of communication. But with vets for parents, it was only natural that he'd learn his animals first."

"He gets his genius from his mother," Madison said as she walked out of the room. "Come with me, Rachel, and we'll see what's wrong with Mrs. Puddleduck."

Rachel followed her outside and into the building that housed their clinic. "How did you know her name?"

"You know how it is in a place like Morgan's Point," Madison said with a smile. "Everybody knows everything about everyone."

Rachel returned her smile. "I guess that's just one of the drawbacks of living in a small town."

"Actually, it's one of the advantages. We have no need for a dog pound, or dog catchers. If an animal gets out, someone who knows the owner is going to take the dog home. Same thing with kids. Kathy Barker's two-year-old climbed over their back gate and wandered a few blocks away last summer. Mr. Jamison found him and started making phone calls."

Madison carefully examined the duck, and kept up a steady stream of conversation. "He was only gone ten minutes before Mr. Jamison took him home. Kathy was still in the backyard looking for him. If that had happened in the city, there's no telling what kind of person might have picked up that child. Even if it had been a concerned neighbor, they'd have called the police and the child would've been taken to the station. It might have been hours before he was returned."

"I suppose it can be an advantage in a situation like that," Rachel admitted.

"I love this little town. There's enough to worry about when you're a parent, but at least here we know our kids can grow up and play in a safe environment."

"These last weeks have been my first exposure to small-town living. But you've probably already heard that, haven't you?"

"As a matter of fact, I have. I don't even know why we have a weekly paper. Word of mouth is a much more effective method of relaying news." Madison finished looking over Mrs. Puddleduck who lay quietly on the exam table. "When did you first notice her symptoms?"

"This evening, about seven. Mother was with her this afternoon and I'm sure she would have mentioned it if she'd noticed any strange behavior."

"This little baby's pretty sick. She has an upper respiratory infection. I'm glad you brought her right over. The sooner we treat it, the faster she'll get well."

Rachel frowned. "Is that bad?"

"Only if it's neglected." Madison opened a cabinet and deftly filled a syringe. "I'll give her an injection tonight and give you some medicine to put in her drinking water. She'll be back to her old self in a few days."

"Too bad," Rachel muttered. "She bites me whenever she gets a chance."

"Just keep giving her the medicine until it's gone."

"I will," Rachel promised.

"Call me in a couple of days and let me know how she's doing. I don't think she will, but if she should take a turn for the worse, get her back in here right away."

Mrs. Puddleduck didn't move a muscle when Madison gave her the shot, but she did stare accusingly at Rachel throughout the ordeal.

Madison put some towels in a box and gently laid Mrs. Puddleduck inside. "She might be more comfortable if you don't handle her too much. If Lydia wants to bring her inside, tell her I said she's better off in her natural environment. Air-conditioning might aggravate her condition."

"Thanks, Madison, I really appreciate it." Rachel dug into her purse for her checkbook. "How much do I owe you?"

"I'll send you a bill." Madison waved her hand dismissively. "Let's go inside and see how the guys are doing. They're pretty good baby-sitters separately, but when they're together they get to talking and forget to keep an eye on the kids."

"It must be difficult to balance a career and a family," Rachel commented as she picked up the box and carried it gingerly to the door.

"Not really. Bill and I share everything. One of us covers the clinic, so the other can be with the babies. We take turns going out on emergency calls."

"Most of my married female employees and colleagues complain that their husbands don't help them at all. They expect the women to work and help with the expenses, but when it comes to home and children, they're on their own."

"I read somewhere that less than twenty percent of the husbands of working wives help with housework and kids. But Bill's not like that," Madison said with a grin. "We met in vet school and when we realized things were getting serious, we discussed the important issues. We made all the big decisions before we married."

"Bill must be an extraordinary man."

"Most of the time." Madison laughed as they walked into the house again. "But he's still a man and that's somewhat of a handicap to him."

They were still laughing when they entered the kitchen and found Bill chopping vegetables at the counter. Joe was seated in a kitchen chair with the baby asleep in his arms. Madison kissed Bill and pinched his cheek. "I wouldn't trade my Bill for anything. Except maybe a new calf-puller."

Her husband grinned to show what a good sport he was about her teasing. "She's amiable enough now, but wait until she tastes what I did to her enchilada casserole recipe."

"I won't complain," Madison promised. "He's always trying to get out of his turn in the kitchen by overspicing the food. What he doesn't know is that I like things spicy."

"I knew that, you little hot tamale," Bill said with mock suggestiveness. "I just hate to see you get discouraged because I'm the better cook."

"That'll be the day," Madison said as she ducked a flying dish towel.

"What we need are impartial judges." Bill turned to Rachel. "Why don't you two have dinner with us tonight and you can give us a verdict on the casserole?"

Rachel glanced at Joe and he shook his head in a barely discernible manner. As much as he liked Madison and Bill, he'd hoped to spend the evening alone with Rachel. This was supposed to be their first date and he still had to prove to her that she had no reason to be afraid of him. When she quickly looked away, he knew what her answer would be.

Rachel liked the young couple and accepting their kind invitation was a perfect excuse not to be alone with Joe. "We wouldn't want to impose...."

"Nonsense, you'd be helping us out," Madison replied. "Bill always makes so much that if you don't stay, I'll have to eat this stuff for a week. Please stay."

Joe's gaze was questioning, so Rachel said, "Well, Joe, how about it?"

All eyes turned his way and he shrugged. "Looks like we're staying." He carefully shifted the baby to his shoulder and stood up. "I'm going to put Sara to bed. I think she's down for the night."

Rachel was amazed by the ease with which Joe handled the tiny baby. His big hands patted her gently as he swayed from side to side. Had he learned to do that, or was he a natural with children?

"Did Bill change her before she fell asleep?" Madison asked.

"Certainly," her husband replied. "Joe wouldn't take her until I did."

"That's not true, Madison. I merely mentioned that she might need a clean diaper after chugging down a hefty ten ounces of formula." He walked toward the hallway. "I've baby-sat the Toxic Avenger many times and I know this kid. And you might want to check on Davey. I haven't heard a peep out of him in the last five minutes."

"Bill," Madison said with a sigh.

"I'm on my way," her husband replied as he raced down the hall.

"Can I do something to help?" Rachel asked.

"No, but thanks for offering. I just checked and there's nothing left to do. Let's go into the living room and chat."

Rachel sat in the easy chair, moving toys and books out of the way first. She silently congratulated herself on her choice of seating. When the men joined them, Joe wouldn't be able to sit beside her. His nearness always unhinged her somehow and she feared she'd be especially susceptible to him tonight. There was something extra charming about a man who was tender with children and animals.

"How long have you been married?" she asked Madison.

"Almost three years. Our anniversary is next week," the other woman said. "We wanted children right away, and it wasn't as if we were just starting out. We met at school, fell in love and lived together for three years before we got married."

Rachel leaned forward and lowered her voice. "So, you knew right away that Bill was the man for you?"

"Are you kidding?" Madison laughed. "We fought like cats and dogs. I had my life all mapped out. As soon as I graduated I was going back home to open a rural practice. I was a country girl from Texas and Bill was a spoiled brat from Southern California. If he had any plans, they ran along the lines of taking care of rich people's neurotic poodles."

"How did you ever get together if you held such different views?" Rachel wondered aloud. If there was a secret involved, she wanted to know it.

"Chemistry." Madison smiled reminiscently. "We couldn't keep our hands off each other. Maybe that's why we've had two kids in three years."

Rachel smiled. Maybe there was more to chemistry than she'd thought. It had worked for Madison and Bill. "Were you ever afraid that you'd never work out your differences?"

"Sure. That's why we fought all the time." Madison lowered her voice. "Bill didn't want to fall in love with me any more than I wanted to fall in love with him. We were in the same study group and we always took opposite sides on everything. Finally, one of the guys in the group suggested that we kiss and make up so we could get on with the more important issues. In the meantime, they all got up and left us alone."

Rachel was caught up in the story. "So did you kiss and make up?"

"Not right away." Madison grinned. "I was so embarrassed to be alone with him in his apartment, that I began accusing him of deliberately trying to goad me into an argument. One minute we were yelling and screaming at each other and the next, we were in each other's arms. That night is burned in my memory forever."

Rachel worried about her new friend. "You took a big chance. What if he decides someday that he made a mistake by giving up his dreams of California?"

"That dream belonged to his parents. Bill hadn't really planned that far ahead. Florida was his decision and I agreed. But I would have followed him anywhere."

Rachel didn't bother to point out the obvious flaws in such an arrangement. It always came down to the vulnerability of a woman in love. Madison had left herself wide open for pain in one form or another. It was a bad idea for a woman to build her life around a man.

"I see," Rachel said softly.

"No, you don't," Madison said with a good-natured grin. "But you will someday."

Several more minutes passed before Bill came into the room carrying Davey. He plopped down on the sofa next to his wife. "I'll give you three guesses where this guy was, and the first two don't count."

Madison shook her head. "In the bathroom, playing in the toilet."

Davey pouted up at his mother and she reached out her arms. The child resettled himself in her lap. "It's okay. Daddy was supposed to watch you and he knows better than to leave the bathroom door open."

Bill slid his arm around his wife's shoulders. "I told Joe you'd blame me. So he volunteered to help with Davey's bath and shampoo, while I did latrine duty."

"Where is Joe?" Madison asked.

Bill looked a little sheepish. "Changing into dry clothes."

Joe stood in the Taylors' bathroom, looking at himself in the mirror. This getup was a far cry from the freshly pressed suit he'd worn over here, but it would have to do. The denim shorts and T-shirt were not what he would have chosen to wear to spend the evening with Rachel, but he didn't have much choice. The doc was considerably shorter than him and his slacks would have looked like high-water pants.

Joe never should have used that toy to distract Davey from the shampooing. Who would have thought one little plastic boat could hold enough water to soak the front of his pants?

When he entered the living room, he saw that he had two choices. He could sit at the other end of the long sofa, or he could perch on the arm of Rachel's chair. He chose the latter.

Rachel refused to draw attention to herself by showing her dismay when Joe propped himself on the arm of her chair. She kept her attention on the others in the room and ignored him.

"I'm sorry about your suit, Joe," Madison said. "I hope it's not ruined."

He draped an arm across the back of the chair, careful not to touch Rachel in any way. She looked nervous enough to bolt for the door. "Don't worry about it, it's only water."

Rachel wished she didn't have such an extraordinary peripheral view of Joe's long, tanned leg. She clasped her hands tightly in her lap to keep from running her hand over his muscled thigh, densely forested with golden hair. She could smell the light fragrance he wore, could feel the vibrations of his voice when he spoke. She'd never been so aware of a man in her life.

She was so wrapped up in her thoughts of Joe, she almost missed the comment Bill directed to her. "There's considerable speculation around town regarding your plans, Rachel."

"There is?"

"Some folks say you'll hightail it back to Jacksonville as soon as Lydia's up to snuff. Others argue that Lydia is fit enough now and that isn't why you're still here. They're betting you stay for good."

"Mother still needs me. It's true that she's recuperating physically, but I'm concerned about the new life-is-short-so-go-for-the-gusto attitude she's developed since the accident."

"I think her new hairdo is cute," Madison put in.

"Oh, it would be. On a teenager," Rachel agreed.

Madison looked thoughtful. "I think the changes your mother is making are understandable. When a person comes so close to dying or being bedridden for the rest of her life, she's bound to see things differently."

"I don't think you need to be concerned, Rachel." Joe had mixed feelings about reassuring her. He didn't want her to worry unnecessarily, nor did he want her to be relieved enough to go back to Jacksonville. "It's not as if Lydia has taken up with a gigolo and run off to the Riviera to gamble away her life's savings."

"Joe's right," Bill agreed. "Ernie's a great guy and well thought of in this town. He's a good steadying influence for your mother."

"I think Mother's beginning to think he's a little too steady," Rachel said. "Just the other day she mentioned that Ernie lacked spunk."

Madison laughed. "I know what she means. I like spunk in a man, too."

"Hold that thought," Bill said with a comic wiggling of his brows. "Let's eat. I can see I'm going to need my strength."

The casserole was heavily spiced, but neither Madison or Bill seemed to mind. Joe followed Rachel's example by eating sparingly of the main course and concentrating on the salad.

Rachel sipped freely of the dark wine Bill served with the meal. She hadn't wanted to have so much fun with Joe, but she couldn't remember ever feeling quite as mellow as she did that evening. The four of them working and laughing together made a quick job of clearing the table and loading the dishwasher.

"It's still early. Why don't we play a game of cards?" Bill suggested.

Joe shook his head. "We really should get Mrs. Puddleduck back before Lydia goes home and finds her missing."

Now why hadn't she thought of that? Rachel wondered. What was wrong with her? Not once, since depositing her mother's pet in the entry hall, had she given a thought to that duck. Was she heartless after all? Bill's question about her plans to return to Jacksonville had given her pause. Was she still in Morgan's Point for some reason besides her mother? Was Joe Morgan that reason?

She managed to shake out of her introspection long enough to bid a warm farewell to Bill and Madison. She agreed to call Madison soon so they could get together for lunch.

Joe glanced at Rachel as he backed out of the driveway. He'd planned to take her to dinner at a trendy seafood restaurant and club in a neighboring town. He'd heard the food was excellent, the service was impeccable and the band was good. All the things she expected to be available only in the city. His plan was to show her that good things sometimes came in small packages.

However, he'd enjoyed the evening spent with his friends. Observing the special give-and-take of the Taylors' marriage made him realize that equality between husband and wife made for a much healthier relationship. If anything ever happened to Bill, Madison would not be in the position Lydia Fox had been in following her husband's death.

He'd been wrong to think that a woman should live her life for her husband. A man and woman should share their lives with each other, independent and whole. The discovery made Joe happy and he wondered aloud what Rachel had thought of the Taylors.

"I think they're extremely warm and friendly," she said. "Their children are beautiful."

"So," he asked casually as he watched the road, "do you like kids?"

The question surprised her. "Well, sure. It's hard not to like something that cute."

"Have you ever thought about having any yourself?"

Rachel wasn't sure where the questions were leading, but it was obviously dangerous territory. "I've thought about it."

She seem unwilling to volunteer more, so Joe dropped the subject. They were quiet during the rest of the short ride to her mother's house. When they arrived, he got out of the car and opened the door for her.

"I'll carry Mrs. Puddleduck around to the backyard while you go inside and turn on the lights," he told her.

She did so and stepped out onto the patio just as Joe was going out through the gate. "Are you leaving?"

"Yes."

"Weren't you planning to say goodbye?"

"Sure." Joe wanted to stay, but didn't really expect an invitation.

Stalling, she asked, "Where's Puddleduck?"

"I put her in her house. She settled right down."

"I appreciate your help tonight. I'm not sure I would have managed so well if you hadn't been here."

"You were all set to beat down poor Bertie Caldwell's door," he reminded her.

"I guess I think the worst of people."

"That comes from living in the city all your life. But we both know you would have managed just fine on your own. You're the most capable woman I know."

"I'm glad I didn't have to." Rachel gave him what she hoped was an inviting look, then crossed the distance between them. "I think I'll sit out here until Mother gets home so I can tell her about Puddleduck."

"That's a good idea." Rachel was a puzzle to Joe. She was unlike any woman he'd ever known. He thought he recognized a "come hither" look in her eyes, but so far he hadn't had much luck reading her signals. Did she want him to stay or go? He released the latch and leaned his shoulder against the gate.

"What do you want, Rachel?"

She wasn't sure; all she knew was what she didn't want. She didn't want to be left alone with her thoughts. She didn't want to question all the rules she'd made in her life. She didn't want to fall in love with Joe Morgan.

"Nothing," she said finally. Which is exactly what she had to look forward to when she returned to Jacksonville. Nothing at all. "I just wanted to say that I enjoyed this evening very much."

"I'm glad. Does that mean you'd be willing to try again? Maybe next time we can have that dinner date I planned for us."

"I'm game if you are."

"Can I call you tomorrow?"

"Please do."

Joe was very aware of Rachel's beauty and of the way the moonlight filtered through her dark hair, highlighting the pale ivory of her skin. He wanted nothing more than to pull her into his arms and kiss her deeply. The wary look in her eyes warned him away.

"I guess I should say good-night," he murmured, still entranced by the woman and the soft, fragrant night that surrounded her.

"Well . . . good night," she whispered.

After he slipped through the gate, Rachel wandered over to the chaise longue and sat there with tears dripping down her face. She wasn't sure if Joe was in love with her or not, but she was certain of one thing. She could have him if she wanted him. She'd seen that in his eyes before he'd turned away.

She also knew something else. She'd better be careful. Joe Morgan was not a man to be taken lightly.

Chapter Nine

Joe felt pretty low when he left Rachel and went home. He tossed restlessly in bed until sometime in the night when he recalled a remark Bill had made earlier in the evening. When Joe had mentioned the troubles he had with Rachel, his friend had pointed out that it was often the differences between a man and woman that made a relationship exciting.

There in the bathroom, with little Davey splashing in the water, Bill had clapped Joe on the back and told him that it was amazing how many differences could be resolved with love and compromise.

Before drifting off to sleep, Joe finally admitted that he was deeply and irrevocably in love with Rachel Fox. He wasn't convinced that love was something one "fell into." More likely, it was something that evolved gradually out of that initial physical attraction.

It had to be love. Only love could make the very qualities he had at first condemned in Rachel, so appealing now. With time, he'd come to admire her independence and self-sufficiency. He'd once thought it would be nice to be needed, but how much nicer to be wanted for himself and not for what he could provide. He'd believed dependence meant security; in fact, it was just the opposite. The burden of being another person's reason for living was a responsibility he no longer wanted.

No wonder she'd kept him at arm's length. She knew she could never be the kind of woman he had thought he wanted. Somehow, he had to let her know that his needs had changed and he wouldn't let a little thing like her out-and-out rejection stand in his way. First thing in the morning, he'd go over to her mother's house and talk to her.

He was encouraged in his plan because he had good reason to suspect she harbored similar feelings for him. Didn't her lips melt beneath his whenever they kissed? And every time he held her in his arms, she returned each caress. Rachel was a strong-willed woman, but when he touched her, she lost control and responded to him as no one ever had before.

"Okay," he said to his mirror image as he lathered shaving cream over his face the next morning. "So Rachel's as hot for you as you are for her. Be prepared for the fact that love might not have anything to do with her feelings."

He carefully stroked the razor over the skin beneath his nose. The fact that he didn't nick that hazardous area seemed a good omen. He grinned. "Of course she loves me. She just doesn't know it yet."

A loud knock on the door caused Joe to jerk and open a small cut in his cheek. "Mr. Morgan, sir? It's me, Lilly."

Joe grabbed a piece of toilet tissue and stuck it to the bleeding wound as he opened the door. Striving to make his voice light, he asked the woman, "Lilly! What are you doing here?"

Lilly Dunlop bobbed from side to side, trying to peer over his shoulder. No doubt she was trying to see who he'd been talking to. "Why, sir, I've been coming here every Saturday since you moved in, to clean and do the laundry. You didn't forget, did you?"

Joe glanced at his watch. It was indeed Saturday. How could he have forgotten a routine of over five years? Apparently, love also had the power to turn one's brain to mush.

"I heard you had a date last night and I didn't want to walk in on anybody.... Oh, my goodness, sir, that's a nasty cut. Did you do that shaving?"

No, he wanted to tell the well-meaning busybody, I did that when you tried to pound the door down. Instead, he replied, "I guess I wasn't paying attention."

"Preoccupied, huh, sir?" she said knowingly. "I swear I heard you talking in here."

Joe pushed the door fully open so the little housekeeper could see for herself that he wasn't hiding anyone in the room. "I was practicing a speech."

Lilly frowned at him. "What speech would that be? I haven't heard a word about it."

"It isn't actually a speech, I'm just making a few remarks to open the Follies. Do you need to talk to me about something else, Lilly? I'm kind of in a hurry."

"Is it okay for me to start in your bedroom? Normally, I like to work my way downstairs, but if you prefer I could start downstairs today."

"There's no need for you to change your routine because I overslept. Why don't you go downstairs and have a cup of coffee? I'll be out of here in three minutes, five, max."

Lilly raised one gray eyebrow and looked at him dubiously. "Take your time," she said, obviously in a snit. "Take all the time you need, Mayor. Don't mind me."

Joe hurried to finish shaving and scraped his chin in the process. Knowing Lilly and her fondness for gossip, he realized that even before the lunch menus hit the soda bar at the drugstore, it would be all over town that he'd been talking to himself.

When he left the house, Joe didn't go straight to Rachel's as he'd planned. He decided to go to Cusak's. He waited until the customers cleared out before approaching the pharmacist. "Clay, I need to talk to you."

Clay finished counting pills for a prescription, before looking up. "I can't help you, Joe. I'm the last person to plead your case with Rachel, anyway. I've been crazy about her myself for years."

"What are you talking about?"

"Didn't you come here to ask me for advice on what to do about Rachel?"

"No. Well, yes. How did you know I was crazy about her?"

"Hattie told me."

Joe threw his hands up. "What does Hattie know about it?"

"Only what she heard from Dottie who heard it from your housekeeper. Rumor has it that you were talking to Rachel in your bathroom and she wasn't even there." When Clay finally looked up, he asked, "Why are you wearing spots of tissue on your face?"

Joe rolled his eyes. "I cut myself shaving."

"You need a good styptic pencil. We've got some right over there."

Joe waved his arm. "Never mind that. You know Rachel as well as anyone, so I want you to tell me everything there is to know about her. I need to know what makes her tick."

"That would take a little longer than I have to spare right now, Joe. Rachel's a complex woman."

A customer came in, dropped off a couple of prescriptions and said he'd be back in the afternoon to pick them up. Joe waited until the door closed behind the man; then he said, "Okay, so give me the abridged version."

Clay busied himself behind the counter. "Maybe you should ask Rachel."

"Come on, Clay. I need your help."

"Well, I guess it won't hurt to tell what's common knowledge. Rachel's father died suddenly and unexpectedly. He was only forty-eight and didn't know he had a heart condition. He had life insurance, but he'd borrowed against it for the girls' educations. There was hardly enough left over for the family to give him a decent funeral and they had nothing to live on."

"Didn't they own their home?"

"Yeah, but they had recently remodeled and there was a mortgage. Lydia lived for her children, but mostly for Harvey Fox. When he died, leaving her virtually penniless, she was a basket case. Rachel was a freshman in college and Molly was in med school."

"Lydia told me she took his death pretty hard."

"She spent most of her time crying. I think seeing her mother fall apart like that was harder on Rachel than losing her father. The family was in trouble and Rachel told me she was the only one who could get them out. She did a quick study on the real-estate market, talked to a savvy agent and put the house up for sale. She rented an apartment, moved the most valuable pieces of furniture into it and sold the rest. She worked fast—the house was virtually empty the day of the funeral, the same day Molly arrived home.

"I don't think Lydia ever knew about the argument the girls had that day, but I'll never forget it. Molly accused Rachel of being cold and unfeeling."

"And Rachel gave as good as she got."

"Not really, she just stood there and agreed with her. She told Molly that she was going to be as cold and unfeeling as she could manage to be for the rest of her life. Then she told her sister to start applying for grants and loans for the rest of her education, because the free ride was over."

Clay shook his head. "The next day I proposed to Rachel, magnanimously offering to quit college and get a job. I vowed I'd take care of her, but she just looked at me as if I'd asked her to suck pond scum. Her exact words escape memory, but the gist of it was that she would never be dependent on a man for her happiness or her security as long as she lived."

Joe sighed. "That explains a lot of things."

"Do you know about the guy she was engaged to?"

Joe looked up, his shock apparent.

"I guess not," Clay said with a grimace. "Me and my big mouth."

Joe thought back to the day they'd visited Sinola. Rachel had told him she'd never been in love. She hadn't mentioned a fiancé. Since an engagement rarely slipped one's mind, she had obviously avoided telling him about it. "I didn't know."

"Maybe it's not my place to fill you in." Clay hesitated. "I've probably said more than I should have already."

"Look, I need to understand Rachel if I'm ever going to get through to her. Come on, Clay, help me."

"That's a big favor, Joe. You're asking me to help you win the woman I love."

Joe looked at the younger man seriously. "I thought that was just talk. Do you really love her?"

"A twenty-five-year habit is hard to break. But no, I guess what I feel for Rachel is not the kind of love you feel for her. Besides, she'll never see me as anything but a brother."

"Tell me about the fiancé."

"About three years after her father died, Rachel got engaged to a man Lydia didn't approve of. She wanted me to try and talk Rachel out of marrying the guy, but I was feeling pretty rejected myself and couldn't do much good."

"After what you've just told me, I'm surprised she let herself love someone so soon."

"I never said she loved him."

"But..." Maybe Rachel had been honest that day at Trader's Oak. Maybe she'd never loved the guy.

"The boyfriend came from old money and wanted Rachel for all the wrong reasons. He was an odd bird. I don't know what her agenda was, but I suspect she knew she'd never really have to let him get close. He jilted her a month before the wedding and ran off with his lover."

Joe shook his head. "She must have been devastated. To trust someone and then have him leave her for another woman like that."

"I said he ran off with his lover. I didn't say it was another woman."

Joe didn't want to hear anymore, but Clay wasn't finished. "I only told you this, Joe, because I don't want to see Rachel hurt again. She's a very special person and she needs someone to understand her. I'm probably her best friend, but she keeps me at arm's length while acting like we're cozy buds. She's got a lot of love inside her, but she's never learned how to give it.''

"I know. I love her, Clay, and it's driving me crazy."

Clay nodded. "I'll tell you one thing and you can take it to the bank. The friend approach won't work—I've been using it for years. It never got me anywhere."

"Thanks, Cusak."

"Don't thank me yet." Clay shrugged. "It's every man for himself. Maybe I'll get lucky and she'll bounce into my arms on the rebound."

Leaving the drugstore, Joe went across the street to his office. He locked the door behind him and pulled down the shades. Sitting in his leather chair, he propped his feet on the desk and leaned back. He had to think this through.

After what he'd just learned, he had doubts about the plan he'd formulated earlier. Even if his suspicions were correct and Rachel loved him, it was unlikely that she would admit it easily.

Admission was the key. She had to acknowledge her feelings before she could learn to accept them. But as any number of self-help groups advocated, to solve a problem, one had to first admit there *was* a problem. And he still wasn't sure how to go about getting her to admit she loved him.

He needed to follow Clay's advice about not trying to be her friend. At the same time, he needed to set up a nonthreatening situation in which they could share their feelings.

Joe picked up the phone and dialed Rachel's number. When she told him she couldn't spend the afternoon with him, he reminded her of the pact they'd made the night of the tryouts.

"I have work to do, Joe."

"No, you don't. It's Saturday. We're just going for a little drive in the country."

"To do what?" she wanted to know.

"Oh, I don't know. Maybe we'll chase butterflies."

Chase butterflies! Rachel didn't know why she had agreed to such a thing, but she had and she would have to make the best of a bad bargain.

They took a primitive road that cut across the Cypress Knoll property and drove for several minutes before Joe pulled the Jeep over and parked under a shady tree.

"What do we do first?" she asked as she climbed out.

He smiled at her. "First we have lunch."

"I'm not particularly hungry," she told him when she remembered what had happened at their last picnic. She wasn't about to serve herself up à la carte on a plaid blanket again.

Joe pulled a basket out of the back. "I didn't eat breakfast, and I'm starving. I get cranky when I miss too many meals in a row."

"Okay, first we eat," she relented. "Are the butter-flies far from here?"

Joe tossed her the blanket, shaded his eyes and squinted into the distance. "Not far."

She spread the blanket on the ground and sat down near a corner. "I didn't know you were interested in lep-idopterology, Joe."

"I beg your pardon?"

"Butterfly collecting," she clarified. "I didn't know you did that."

"There's lots of things you don't know about me, Rachel."

That was an understatement. "What are we having this time?"

"I hope you like ham," he said. He put the basket in the middle of the blanket and sat down across from her. He pulled out the food. "Ham sandwiches, black olives, cupcakes and wine."

"You hit all the food groups, huh?"

"I was in a hurry."

Rachel laughed, and as they ate she gave him a progress report on Mrs. Puddleduck's recovery.

"How did your mother handle it?"

She shrugged. "Amazingly well."

"Lydia's a strong woman."

"Is that how you see her? Really?"

Joe thought about it. "I've only known her for five years, but yes, I think she's strong. She went through a lot of pain and frustration after her accident and she coped."

"I've always thought of her as vulnerable and dependent. When my father died, she just wilted. She was so bound up in her grief and fears, that I worried she'd never get out again."

"She's a survivor. So are you."

"I guess I am."

Joe gestured at the other half of her sandwich, lying forgotten on the plastic wrap. "Aren't you going to finish that?"

"No, I'm saving room for a cupcake. Do you want it?"

"Thanks. I told you I was hungry."

"What about your parents, Joe? Mother said they moved to a condo in Jacksonville three years ago."

"Actually it's on the outskirts. That's as close to town as Dad would consent to be. He didn't want to move at all, but Mom insisted. She wanted to be closer to the doctor because of his heart."

"I'm sorry. I didn't know your father had a bad heart."

"He doesn't now. Four years ago, he had open-heart surgery, a triple bypass. He followed the doctor's orders to quit smoking and stays on his 'healthy heart' diet. The doctor says he's fine now, but Mother refuses to believe it."

"That must be hard on your father."

"Are you kidding? He loves it. I've never seen a bigger baby than my dad." He unwrapped a cupcake and handed one to Rachel. "Mom says all men are babies, but I disagree."

"Oh, well, you would." She took a bite of the gooey treat and savored the chocolate assault on her taste buds.

"I'm self-sufficient," he protested. "I can cook, I can clean and I can sew on my own buttons."

"I thought you had a housekeeper," she chided.

"I said I could do all those things. I didn't say I liked doing them. Besides, Lilly was a hand-me-down from my parents. I inherited her. I could get along without her, but she needs the income to supplement her retirement."

She laughed and he marveled at the softness that transformed her. "I don't expect a woman to wait on me hand and foot."

"Funny, I had you pegged as being a bit more chauvinistic than that."

Joe smiled. So she had been thinking about him, imagining what he was like. Maybe he even figured in her daydreams. That was something in his favor. "I want to be loved. Who doesn't? But I don't need mothering." He polished off the cupcake and licked his fingers. "I'd make someone a good house-husband."

Rachel laughed. "Too bad you can't bear children, or I'm sure you'd have been snatched up long ago."

"It doesn't seem fair, does it?"

"What?" she asked with a teasing grin. "That you haven't been snatched up yet?"

"No, that women are referred to as the weaker sex. I think they're actually the stronger of the sexes. Bill and I joked about this before, but I doubt if any man would willingly bear children even if he could."

"Did Bill offer to do the deed for Madison?"

Joe chuckled. "When Madison was in labor with Davey, he told her he would gladly trade places with her if he could. I believe she offered to scratch his eyes out and have him tossed out of the delivery room on his ear."

"Would you?"

He shook his head. "I don't know. I'd like to say yes, but what if a magic genie popped up and granted that wish? I think I'd run for the hills as fast as my legs would carry me."

Rachel grinned. "So, you believe in such things as magic genies?"

"I've never seen any. How about you?"

"Never," she said softly. "But then I gave up wishing for things a long time ago. It's been my experience that if you want something, you have to work for it."

Joe could believe that. He certainly had his work cut out for him.

"Look, Joe," she whispered softly, pointing at a wildflower near the base of a nearby tree. "What is that?"

Joe squinted. "It looks like a butterfly."

"I know that, silly. What kind is it?"

He was caught, unless he could bluff his way out. He stared at it a few seconds, then said, "I believe that's a yellow-winged Habius Corpi."

Rachel looked at him doubtfully. "I think you made that up."

"I think you have good instincts."

"You lied to me," she accused.

"No, I said we would chase butterflies, I never professed to being an expert. You just assumed that part."

"Then get off your butt and on your feet, fella. That's a butterfly—let's chase it."

He was panting and begging for mercy half an hour later. "I've been tried, convicted and punished. Can we stop now?"

"I guess I've had enough enjoyment for one day," she decided. "You can take me home."

Joe wasn't ready for the date to come to an end. "Do you mind if we just sit in the shade and cool off for a few minutes?"

Rachel collapsed on the blanket and leaned against the tree trunk, while Joe lay on his back, his arms outflung.

"I'll pour us some wine as soon as I catch my breath," he said, panting.

"You're not that tired. You're not even breathing hard," she admonished him. "I know what your problem is."

Joe's problem was being in such close proximity to Rachel all afternoon without being able to express his love. He grinned and rolled over toward her, propping his head on his hand. "If you even mention the aging process, you'll be sorry."

Rachel returned his grin as she poured their wine. "I'm not one to make rude comments about anyone's age. You overate and now all you want to do is rest."

"Now that isn't quite right," he said. "I also want to talk. Part of our agreement was that we would get to know each other better. To do that, we'll have to clarify some of the preconceived notions we have about each other."

"What do you want to know?" she asked guardedly. She pulled her knees to her chest and stared at her feet. "I refuse to tell you my shoe size."

He gently clasped her ankle, and she took a deep breath. She'd been waiting for him to touch her all afternoon. Several times when they'd stopped to admire something, their heads close, she'd been sure he was going to kiss her. But at the last moment, with the need shimmering between them, Joe had stepped back and continued their nature hike. She'd known he was a man of his word, but she wished now that he hadn't promised not to take advantage of her.

He unlaced her shoe, discarded it, then rolled down her sock and slipped it off, too. Her pulses pounded with excitement as he ran his fingers down the length of her foot.

"When I was in high school, I worked in my uncle's shoe store. I know what size shoe you wear," he said in a husky tone. His fingers cupped her heel and then his palm slid up the sole of her foot to massage her toes. She finished her wine and leaned her head against the tree trunk, totally relaxed.

"You do?" Rachel breathed out the words. When had the bones in that foot dissolved?

"What kind of man do you want to marry?" he asked softly.

"You really cut to the chase, don't you?"

"The witness will answer the question," he said in gruff judge voice.

Someone who makes me feel the way you do, were the words that immediately sprang to mind; however, she said, "He'd have to be understanding about my career."

Joe sat up, and removed her other shoe and sock. "In what way?"

"I would never give it up. No matter what, my career comes first."

He poured another cup of the fruity wine and handed it to her. Then his strong fingers began caressing her other foot.

"Aren't you going to have some, too?" she asked.

He shook his head. "I'm the designated driver."

She took a drink, then leaned back again, closing her eyes. The day was warm, but a cool breeze wafted over her heated skin. She breathed deeply of the verdant fragrance of the woods. Cicadas were busy doing their thing in the tall grass and birds chirped in the trees. Maybe nature wasn't so bad, when taken in small doses.

"Supposing this man was supportive of your career," Joe said. "Would you take time out occasionally from your busy schedule to spend time with him and the kids?"

"What kids?"

"Don't you want children someday?"

She pictured herself holding a baby, one with twinkling brown eyes like Joe's. "Maybe one. I wouldn't have time for more. Do you want children?"

"I want at least two. Being an only child is not all it's cracked up to be. I'd like to have more, but I'd settle for two."

She remembered how he'd been with the Taylor children. "You'll be a good father. On the other hand, probably won't make much of a mother. I'm too self centered."

"I disagree. A woman as self-centered as you claim to be wouldn't have put her business on hold to take care of her own mother. A self-centered person would have put her in a nursing home or hired someone else to stay with her. Not only that, but with your willpower you can do anything you make up your mind to do."

"I've had my failures. I was engaged once. Did you know?"

"I believe I heard something about that," he replied vaguely.

"He was very successful and he was great fun at a party. I liked him. And he was just as tied to his career as I was to mine. I made some great business contacts through our association."

"But you weren't in love with him."

Rachel laughed. "No. We were friends. We had an arrangement. I wouldn't interfere in his life and he wouldn't interfere in mine. But it wouldn't have worked over the long haul. I'm glad things ended the way they did."

"So am I," he said softly.

"It's lonely out there in the big, cold world."

"It doesn't have to be."

"No," she agreed. "But love complicates everything."

"I think love would give it all more meaning."

Rachel opened her eyes and their gazes connected. "Maybe, but as you have astutely observed from time to time, it scares the hell out of me."

"In what way?"

"I don't want to lose my independence—it was too hard to win. I don't want to subjugate my personality."

"With the right person, you wouldn't have to."

"I'm not so sure about that." Rachel grabbed her shoes and stood up abruptly. "I think I'd better go home now."

"If that's what you want." Things had gotten too personal for Rachel and she wanted to escape. He'd made some progress today. Not much, but some. Given enough time, he was sure he could get through to her.

Rachel was already in the Jeep by the time he gathered up and loaded their things in the back. She was quiet during the drive and when he pulled up in front of Lydia's house, she opened her door quickly.

"There's no need for you to get out, Joe. Thanks for today. I enjoyed it very much."

"I'm glad. What time shall I pick you up tomorrow?"

"Tomorrow?"

"Quality time, remember?"

"I had no idea that courtships were so time-consuming."

"If you want something to work, you've got to work at it," he said cheerfully.

"I can't see you tomorrow, Joe. I have to go to Jacksonville."

"Good. That's where I wanted to take you anyway."

"I need to go over some books at the office. It'll take hours."

"I don't have anything better to do."

"For an attorney/mayor, you sure have a lot of time on your hands."

"I told you before, the pace is slower in Morgan's Point. What time shall I pick you up?"

Rachel was losing control of the situation and it wasn't a feeling she enjoyed. "I'll drive. I'll pick you up at nine-thirty."

"I'll be waiting."

That's what she was afraid of.

Chapter Ten

The next morning, Joe was sitting on the glider on his front porch when Rachel turned the BMW into his driveway. He waved a greeting and she watched admiringly as he approached. Dressed in a pair of pleated khaki slacks and a lightweight denim shirt, he looked casual and well-groomed. No doubt about it, Joe Morgan was a good-looking man.

Her pulse quickened as he slid into the bucket seat beside her and buckled his seat belt. He grinned as he arranged his long legs in the too-small space, and his smile had a therapeutic effect on her. She realized with a jolt that she was anticipating with pleasure spending the day with him.

"Beautiful morning, isn't it? Days like this make you glad to be alive." She didn't know why she felt so exuberant; maybe it was the sun-washed morning. Then again, maybe it was the company.

"You noticed. There's hope for you yet," he said as he gave her hand a gentle squeeze.

It took less than an hour to drive to Jacksonville and they kept up a steady stream of small talk most of the way. Joe filled her in on how this year's Follies were shaping up and advised her that the Miss Cypress Knoll beauty queen had been chosen and would be crowned at the Autumn Festival. As he went on to describe the parade and other planned activities, Rachel suddenly realized that she probably wouldn't be in Morgan's Point when autumn came.

Lydia had recovered as much mobility as she ever would. Despite her criticisms regarding Ernie Baxter's energy level, the couple had spent a lot of time together lately and Rachel felt it wouldn't be long until Lydia accepted his proposal. When they married, there would be no reason for Rachel to stay in Morgan's Point. Far from feeling relieved, she felt dismayed at the prospect of leaving. Of leaving Joe.

"Rachel?" Joe asked when he saw her expression change. Something had disturbed her. "What's wrong?"

"What? Oh, nothing. I was just thinking about something. I'm sorry, what were you saying?"

"It wasn't important," he assured her. He'd seen the faraway look in her eyes as he'd talked about the upcoming festivities. Such things probably weren't as exciting as the gala social events she was used to, but he'd assumed that she was at least interested. Perhaps he'd been wrong. He didn't bring the subject up during the rest of the trip.

The main office of Fox Realty was located in a luxury high-rise building on a busy commercial street in Jacksonville. Constructed of steel and reflecting glass and surrounded by carefully tended palm trees and lush landscaping, it whispered of prestige and style. Rachel's company occupied the east side of the first floor.

"It's pretty quiet around here on Sunday morning," Rachel told Joe after they'd parked and gone inside. "That's when I like to come in and catch up. Later in the afternoon, some of our agents will be in to man the phones and follow up on leads from the weekend open houses we hold."

"Nice place." He looked around at the functional, yet attractive, decor of the office. "Very impressive."

"Thank you." Rachel was proud of the environment she had created at Fox. The color scheme combined off-white with sea green and mauve accents to suggest tranquillity. Clients found the atmosphere relaxing after an exhausting round of house tours and a relaxed client was more likely to make an offer.

Graphic-style prints of tropical fish and other undersea creatures dotted the walls with bold splashes of color. Large plants provided living, green dividers between the desks and afforded individuals with some privacy in the open area. Vibrant silk arrangements of hibiscus and oleander, as well as the white wicker furniture in the reception area, lent a restful, garden atmosphere.

"You really are a success story, Rachel. This is an even bigger operation than I expected. How many people do you employ?"

"Fourteen at the moment. We're not as big as the chains, but we have a reputation for getting the job done." To impress upon him that this was her life and not just her livelihood, she added, "Last year a large company tried to buy me out. It was a very tempting offer, but I turned it down. Without the agency, I wouldn't have anything to do with my time."

Joe could make a few suggestions: get married, have a few babies. His babies. Instead he shrugged and said, "You could travel, dabble in the stock market, even take up deep-sea fishing. Have you never harbored a secret, burning ambition to be a painter or a bag lady?"

Rachel laughed. "No, I can't say that I have. For nine years I've poured every ounce of my energy into getting ahead. I couldn't let up now."

"Why didn't you take the money and start another company?"

"I would have liked the challenge of that, but as part of the deal, I would have had to agree not to open another real-estate office in Jacksonville."

"And the business is in your blood, huh?"

"It's been very good to me. When I first started out, the real-estate market was booming. Anyone with a license could make money if she was willing to hustle."

"Is that why you got into it?"

"At first. When Dad died, I had to put our home on the market. When I saw the kind of commission the agent got, I decided that was the way to go. We needed money fast and it was a means to an end."

"You sound like you have doubts now."

She continued to talk as she showed him into her private office. "It still provides a good income, but maintaining a client list like mine can be a twenty-hour-a-day job. I've lost sales because I'm out of reach right now."

"Do you regret that?"

"Not really," she said, surprised that she meant it. "I think the time I've spent in Morgan's Point has been good for me. It's helped me see things differently and to put my life into perspective."

"I'm glad to hear that, Rachel."

"You're partly responsible for that, you know. You made me slow down and not only smell the flowers, but chase the butterflies along the way. You helped me see that my way isn't the only way. The best way, yes. But not the only way."

"I was hoping you'd see more than that. I want you—"

He was interrupted by the ringing telephone. Rachel took the call and talked to a prospective client as Joe prowled around the room. He noted the many framed awards and plaques hanging on the wall including Businesswoman of the Year, Outstanding Broker—Southern Region and more than one Top Sales recognition. Rachel wasn't exaggerating when she said she put all her energy into her work.

She hung up the phone and apologized for the interruption.

"Your awards are impressive."

"Like I said, I had to work for them. And speaking of work, I need to do some now."

"Take all the time you need. I'll use the receptionist's desk and make a few phone calls while I'm waiting."

Going over the computerized accounts, Rachel saw that her office manager was as efficient as ever. Everything was as it should be; the place ran smoothly even when she wasn't there. Leaning back in her chair, she wondered what her life would have been like if she'd sold the agency when she'd had the chance.

At the time, the idea of getting out of the rat race had been tempting, not because of the money, but because she was tired. She never would have admitted it before, but the weeks in Morgan's Point had shown her that she pushed herself too hard. Since she'd been away from the office, she didn't wake every morning with that queasy, burning sensation in her stomach. After the initial shock had passed, it had actually been pleasant to look in her appointment book and find blank pages.

At first, the lack of structure had been intimidating. But after a few weeks, she'd come to appreciate the freedom that life in Morgan's Point afforded. It was painful to accept, but it was true. The business which was supposed to make her independent had, in fact, enslaved her. Maybe that's what her mother had been trying to tell her all along.

But if not for Fox Realty, what did she have in her life? What would she do without it? She hadn't been completely truthful earlier when Joe had asked her about secret ambitions. She'd once considered writing a how-to book to help people sell their own homes, or one with information for potential buyers. But then what? What would she do with the rest of her empty, lonely life?

No. She had to stop thinking like that. When she got home for good, things would get back to normal. She was only having these thoughts because Joe had planted the seed earlier with his questions about unfulfilled needs. Joe. He was a big part of those unfulfilled needs. He was at the heart of it all.

She glanced around the office she'd so painstakingly furnished. This was all hers and she'd find a way to make it as interesting and challenging as it had been before. Now that she had what she'd always wanted, how could she admit, even to herself, that it wasn't enough?

Finished with her audit of the accounts, she switched off the computer and went out to the reception area.

Joe looked up from the magazine he was leafing through when she entered the room. "Finished already?"

"Yes," she said. "Everything's in good order. My office manager is a jewel. I should seriously consider giving her a big raise."

He glanced at his watch. "Let's go to the mall and have some lunch. You can help me pick out a gift for my mother while we're there."

"Lunch sounds good, but I don't know your mother. I'm afraid I wouldn't be much help in the gift department."

"We'll see."

Over tortilla soup and quesadillas, Rachel said, "When I first met you, I assumed you had political aspirations. That being mayor of Morgan's Point was just a beginning for you."

"What do you think now?"

"I think you're happy right where you are."

"I don't want to be anywhere else," he agreed. "I guess I lack ambition."

"I wouldn't say that. It must feel good to be satisfied with your life."

He wasn't completely satisfied. Something very important was still missing. "I'm reasonably content."

"Have you never harbored a secret, burning desire to be a painter or a bag lady?" she mimicked.

He laughed. "Nope."

"How about a megabuck corporate lawyer, or a champion defender of the people?"

"That's exactly what I had in mind when I finished law school and took my first job. I lived in Miami then. I went to all the right parties and even managed to get engaged to a beautiful attorney whose father was senior partner in the firm we worked for. I was in love with her and with the notion of justice and I thought the two of us would set the world on fire."

"Was she the wrong person you told me about?" she asked.

"The same. I didn't realize how wrong until later."

Rachel was enthralled by his story. She'd assumed Joe had always been a small-town lawyer. "Tell me more."

"I guess you've heard all the lawyer jokes?"

"Which ones?" she asked.

"Like, what do you call it when a plane with five hundred lawyers aboard crashes in the ocean?"

"I don't know. What?"

"A good start."

"I know one. What's the difference between a lawyer and a catfish?"

"One's a scum-sucking bottom dweller and the other's a fish," he deadpanned.

She laughed and several other patrons in the restaurant looked around to see why they were having so much fun.

Joe was warming to his subject. "Why do lawyers carry snakes in their pockets?"

"Why?"

"In case they have to show an ID."

"Oooh, that's harsh."

"Yeah, but if the shoe fits... My former boss was a classic example. Some of the practices he encouraged went against what I thought law was all about."

"You were an idealist," she speculated. "Trying to work with realists."

"Maybe so. When I complained, he made excuses. For a while, and because I didn't want to acknowledge what was going on, I kept quiet. One day, he privately suggested I 'lose' some evidence that I'd uncovered on a defense case I was working on."

"Evidence that wasn't in the best interest of your client?" she guessed.

"It would have sent him to prison for at least twenty years, even with time off for good behavior. I told my boss that ethically I couldn't do what he wanted. He threatened to take me off the case and I told him the firm should withdraw completely because the guy was a guilty jerk."

"And what did he say?"

"He informed me that if I planned to work for him, I'd probably have to compromise my ideals from time to time. The world, he explained, is full of guilty jerks and according to the Constitution, they're all entitled to an attorney."

"What did you do then?"

"I quit. His daughter, my fiancée, tried to talk me out of it. I told Diana I wouldn't go back to the firm. I'd seen enough and I was getting out, going back to Morgan's Point where I belonged. I asked her to come with me, but she refused. Said she'd shrivel up and die in such a backwater place. She was much more ambitious, you see. Not only did she want to be a prominent person, she wanted to be married to one. It would have been beneath her to marry a little Podunk-town lawyer."

"If you loved her, you could have gone to work for a different firm and stayed in Miami."

"You might say I was secretly blackballed."

"Why?"

"The partners thought I told the assistant D.A. where to find the evidence he needed to win his case." At her questioning look, he added, "Hey, I can't help it if the Miami D.A.'s office is on the ball."

"I'm surprised the firm didn't sue."

"They had no proof or they'd have tried to get me disbarred. They were content to see to it that I'd never eat lunch in their town again."

Rachel nodded. He hadn't come right out and said he had helped the other attorney, but she knew he had. Simply put, Joe Morgan was the kind of man who put principles above personal gain. Such old-fashioned integrity was a rare commodity in the world today.

"So you're the last of a dying breed—an honest attorney," she teased.

"There's a lot of us out there," he said modestly.

"Do you ever miss it? The parties, the big cases?" What she really wanted to ask, was if he missed Diana.

"No. Simple pleasures for a simple man. The Chamber Follies are enough excitement for me. And as for the big cases, I may spend my life writing wills and reading abstracts, but at least I can sleep good at night."

Rachel asked the question she hadn't had the nerve to ask earlier. "Do you still miss her?"

"Who? Oh, you mean Diana?" he said. "Not anymore. I told you once that loving the wrong person could break your heart. What I didn't mention was that no heart stays broken forever. Bad love just makes you more grateful when good love comes along."

Rachel sensed that the conversation was about to head down unwanted paths. She finished her ice tea and said brightly, "Let's go shopping."

They finally chose a gift and were waiting for it to be wrapped when Joe asked Rachel if she'd mind stopping by his parents' home to deliver it. When she hedged, he persisted, "Today's her birthday. Be a sport."

"Okay, I can wait in the car."

"You can try, but you'll never get away with that. The folks won't allow it."

"Then, I'll just take you home and you can drive back by yourself."

He glanced at his watch as he picked up the gaily wrapped present. "That would be too late. The party will be over by then."

"What party? You didn't say anything about a party."

Joe took her arm and guided her out to the car. "Every year, Dad gives Mom a surprise party that isn't a surprise. It'll just be a few of their friends and neighbors and whatever single woman they've managed to drag in off the street for me to meet."

Rachel laughed and started the engine. "Trying to set you up, huh?"

"Constantly," he said with a wicked grin. "I have to be careful about how much advance notice I give them when I visit or they have candidates lined up for my inspection."

Following Joe's directions, it didn't take Rachel long to find the address. The house was a sprawling bungalow set in the middle of a lawn so perfect that it could only belong to a retiree with lots of time on his hands.

She parked, but was reluctant to get out. "Will they think it odd if you show up with me in tow?"

"No, I called them from your office. They're thrilled that I actually have a date. They're beginning to think I'm hard to get along with or something."

"I don't think it's a good idea to get their hopes up about us being a couple."

Joe shrugged. "I never said we were. But you know as well as I do, you can't keep parents from jumping to conclusions."

James and Billie Morgan were a delightful couple who made Rachel feel welcome in spite of her misgivings. They seemed genuinely interested in every word she said and took advantage of all opportunities to extol their son's virtues. When Joe and Rachel left, the Morgans made it clear that they expected to see her again. Soon.

"I like your parents," she told him when she dropped him off at home that evening.

"They like you, too. Mom wanted to know why I hadn't given you a ring yet."

She moaned. "I was afraid of that. We gave them the wrong idea."

"Actually I think it's a great idea," he said softly. "How about you?"

"Joe, please. Don't push."

"I withdraw the question," he said in true lawyerly fashion.

"Can I kiss you good-night without anyone jumping to conclusions?" she asked.

"No objection," he said as his lips met hers. The kiss was sweet and hungry for having been denied too long. She sighed and her lips parted. His tongue touched hers and a thrill of desire curled through her, permeating her body like a dense smoke.

Joe didn't think he could take much more of this. Rachel's eager response made him want to carry her, caveman-style, into his bedroom. He wanted to undress her slowly, revealing her beauty to his eyes, inch by inch. He wanted to touch her everywhere, with his hands, his lips. He wanted to feel her soft body wrapped around his; he wanted to hear her cry of release.

That's what he wanted to do. What he actually did, was break the kiss and open his car door. "Do you want to come inside with me?" he asked hoarsely.

"I can't, Joe."

"Then you'd better get out of here before I lose what little control I have left and drag you in."

"Good night, Joe."
"Good night, Rachel."

Starting bright and early the next morning, Rachel made it a point to talk with local residents and find out how they felt about the development of Cypress Knoll. Many of those she spoke with liked the idea, saying they thought the construction of a mall or other commerical venture might entice their children and other kin who had moved away for better job opportunities, to come back to Morgan's Point.

She also asked around to find out what single improvement would benefit the town most. The consensus of her informal poll was that a clinic was badly needed. As it was now, people had to drive over thirty miles to have a baby or to get a bone set. Older residents like James Morgan had had to leave their hometown in order to be close to a medical facility.

Like many rural towns, Morgan's Point hadn't had much luck luring in a new doctor since old Dr. Cooley had retired. If they had the facilities and could guarantee a reasonable income, they might have a better chance of getting a young doctor to come in and establish a practice.

In planning her strategy for the upcoming presentation to the town council, Rachel decided to use the clinic angle. Her goals weren't entirely selfish, after all; her own sister was a doctor who would soon be coming back to Florida to look for a place to hang out her shingle.

If Molly decided to stay, it would be good for Lydia and for the people of Morgan's Point. It would also help assuage the guilt Rachel felt for not being able to prevent Molly from having to go off to Montana in the first place.

Rachel's days were spent working and canvassing, but her evenings were mostly spent with Joe. Over the next couple of weeks, they saw each other often. She tagged along with him to watch the Follies' rehearsals. As stage manager, he gave her a job that was really no more than glorified gopher and yet it made her feel accepted and a part of things.

Standing around backstage, kibitzing with the crew and performers, she got to know the people of Morgan's Point and made many new friends. She also had plenty of opportunities to talk about what the sale of Cypress Knoll could mean to the community.

Since their trip to Jacksonville when Rachel had asked Joe not to push her, he had shown an almost Herculean restraint during the many hours they spent together. She had merely wanted him to stop pushing, not to stop trying altogether, and she sorely missed the hot kisses and desperate fumblings that had characterized their previous encounters.

One night, Rachel and Joe spent a quiet evening playing bridge with Lydia and Ernie. Later they sat on the patio eating homemade ice cream. When the older couple went indoors, Joe stretched his arms above his head and let his right arm rest along the back of the settee he shared with Rachel. He didn't allow his fingers to fondle her hair as he wanted to do. He didn't pull her into his arms and kiss her senseless. He was trying to figure out how to open a topic he didn't really want to discuss.

When he put his arm behind her, Rachel longed to snuggle into his side. She waited for him to touch her shoulder, or caress her neck; she needed a stronger signal if she was to go with her impulses and melt all over him.

"The stars are really bright tonight," he observed.

She nodded. "And there's a big old moon, too."

"Isn't that what they call a lover's moon?"

She sighed. "I wouldn't know."

"I suppose any moon would do if a couple wanted to take advantage of it."

She grinned at him. "I suppose."

He didn't follow her lead and sat quietly, staring into the star-studded sky.

"You're unusually quiet tonight, Joe," she commented after a while. "Is anything wrong?"

"I heard you've been talking to people around town about selling Cypress Knoll."

"It's no secret. We agreed that we'd both present our cases and let the best man win."

"Yeah, we agreed."

"I've kept my end of the bargain. I've spent nearly every evening for two weeks with you. We've gotten to know each other very well."

"Exactly."

"What's that supposed to mean?"

"It means I can't believe you still think development of the area is a good idea."

She was quiet as she considered his words. After a few moments it dawned on her. "This courtship, as you call it, wasn't designed to enhance our relationship at all, was it? You thought you could change my mind by wooing me with sweet words and kisses. That's it, isn't it?"

"I thought I could change your mind by showing you how disastrous it would be to relinquish the wilderness area to development. I thought I could change your mind about going back to Jacksonville. I thought if you got to know the people here and realized what a wonderful place it was, you'd want to stay. But I was wrong. All you're interested in is making a buck and going back to the city."

"You told me you wouldn't use any underhanded tricks against me. Well, this is the most underhanded thing of all. You wanted me to fall in love with you so you could force your opinions on me. You used me."

"I never did."

"Then why do I feel so used?"

Joe had said more than he should have. He hadn't explained things well at all. "I'm sorry, Rachel. I never wanted you to feel that way. You're right. I told you I wouldn't try to sabotage your efforts if you agreed to spend time with me. You did keep your part of the bargain. I'm the one who's being a poor loser because you've nearly swayed the whole town to your way of thinking. That clinic ploy was an artful maneuver."

"It's not a ploy, Joe. This town needs a doctor and it needs a clinic. The sale of Cypress Knoll could provide both. I haven't misrepresented anything. I've been completely aboveboard and I resent your insinuations that I've done otherwise."

She saw a muscle twitch in his cheek before he spoke. "Again, I apologize. I guess I don't like the idea of giving up my dream. I've wanted to see Cypress Knoll preserved ever since I was old enough to understand what would happen if it wasn't."

"It's not over yet. The vote's not in. Why, we haven't even made our presentations to the council."

"According to talk around town, they're as good as convinced. My offer from the government to lease the property for wildlife management can't compare to your million-dollar deal. Like any good businessperson you found the weakness you needed and you exploited it."

"I found out what's needed and found a way to get it."

"The town does need a doctor and clinic. I'll give you that. I just hate to see them get one at the expense of our heritage."

"You're being melodramatic. There are sound ways of reconciling historical preservation and commerce. Have you ever heard of New Market, Maryland?"

"I can't say that I have."

"I visited the town last year when I was in Baltimore for a conference. The town was founded in 1793 and many of the buildings along Main Street still look very much as they did when they were built. The hotels, taverns, barns and inns have been restored, rebuilt and expanded to create one of the most scenic antique shopping areas on the East Coast.

"The town is listed as an historic district by the National Register and the state of Maryland, but it is also a thriving commercial community."

"So what are you getting at?"

"Compromise, Joe. With your help, we can work hand in hand with the developer to ensure that Morgan's Point doesn't become another Sinola. I don't want any hard feelings between us."

"I'll get over it. And I promise to wait until I see what you and this ecologically sound developer have to offer before I pass judgment."

"You won't be sorry, Joe."

"In the meantime, Bill and Madison Taylor invited us to dinner next Thursday night. I know I should have checked with you first, but I told them we'd be there."

Next Thursday? Wasn't something written in her appointment book for that night? Yes, that was the evening she was meeting with Dan Margolian. "I'm sorry, Joe. I have plans already."

"What kind of plans?"

She resented the demand in his tone. "I don't think that's any of your business. This cockamamie courtship of ours doesn't give you the right to monitor all my activities."

He stiffened at her words. "Obviously, this *cockamamie* courtship of ours meant more to me than it did to you."

Why was he using the past tense? Did he consider it over? Despite the heaviness she felt in her chest, Rachel knew it was just as well. Things had gotten too heavy between them anyway. To continue on the course they'd set would only make her ultimate departure from Morgan's Point harder.

"Not that I owe you an explanation, but I'm meeting with the developer that night to show him around town."

"When did you set that meeting?"

"Three weeks ago."

Joe felt the fight go out of him. All the times they were together, in Jacksonville, with his parents, at the rehearsals, she'd been secretly plotting against him. All the times she was kissing him, she'd been stabbing him in the back. Maybe she wasn't the woman he'd thought she was.

No. That was the problem. She was exactly the woman he'd first believed her to be—cool, calculating and ambitious. Interested only in furthering her career.

"The most ironic part of all this is that you don't even need the money you'll make on the sale of Cypress Knoll," he told her. "It's all a game to you."

His words were icy and Rachel felt the sting in her heart. "Joe, that's not true. I admit that at first I wanted to get back at you for beating me that other time. That first day in your office, you made me feel like a desirable woman instead of a businesswoman and I resented that.

"But after I got to know you and the rest of the people here better, I wanted to help them get something they need. I'm planning to donate my commission to the building fund for the clinic if things work out in my favor."

"How generous of you."

"Joe, please. Don't take this so personal."

"I care about you, Rachel. I thought you cared about me. I can't help but take it personal."

"I do care, believe me."

"I'd like to, Rachel. But I'm feeling a little betrayed right now."

"That's not fair! I haven't done anything I didn't have your permission to do. You're the one who's reneging on the bargain. Can't you at least wait until my client makes an offer before you get angry? You might be pleasantly surprised."

"I doubt it. Who is your client, anyway?"

"The Margolian brothers. They've had lots of experience developing property in this part of the state."

Joe got to his feet. "I'm well acquainted with your friends, the Margolian brothers. They're the ones who developed, or should we say raped, Sinola."

Before Rachel could respond to that bombshell, Joe stalked through the side gate and disappeared.

Chapter Eleven

Rachel knew Joe was angry, because he wouldn't take her calls. When she went to his office to talk to him, his secretary told her he wasn't in. She knew he was because she'd been sitting in Perkins' across the street when she saw him enter. When she said as much, Lou Ann apologized for her boss's behavior, saying she had orders not to let Rachel in.

After that, Rachel's pride wouldn't let her try again. If he was so stubborn and hardheaded that he wouldn't listen to reason, then she wasn't going to waste any more time on him. He'd been a pleasant diversion, but they'd both known from the beginning that things could never work out between them. It was better if she just made a clean break.

However, the look of betrayal she'd seen on his face when he found out about the Margolian brothers still haunted her. She would talk to the developers and explain how important it was for their firm to work carefully with the people of Morgan's Point to create an ecologically sound plan. Then she would have something to take to the town council and to Joe Morgan. She'd find satisfaction in showing him he'd been wrong.

On the afternoon of her meeting, she was sitting on the patio waiting for the Margolians and stroking Mrs. Puddleduck who lay placidly in her lap. Rachel couldn't explain it, but the illness had changed the duck's attitude toward her. It no longer tried to nip her at every turn, nor did it squawk furiously whenever she got near. Lydia thought Puddleduck was grateful for Rachel taking her to the vet and saving her life. Rachel thought the fever had burned up a few of the bird's limited brain cells.

Lydia had been out with Ernie all day and when she came in she was all aflutter. "Guess where I've been."

Rachel, who was still depressed over Joe's hostility toward her, made a lackluster response. "Venus?"

"No, silly. Ernie took me to Jacksonville."

"That's nice."

"Don't you want to know why?"

Rachel tried for some enthusiasm. "Why did you go to Jacksonville, Mom?"

"For this!" Lydia thrust her left hand under Rachel's nose and waved it. On her third finger was a ring with a very large pear-shaped diamond.

"Mother!"

"I'm engaged! Isn't it wonderful?"

"Well, yes, if you're sure that's what you want."

"Oh, it is," Lydia gushed. "I was wrong about Ernie. He's so kind and loving. He's also thoughtful and devoted." She blushed and added, "And he's plenty man enough for me."

"Obviously, there's been a few developments since the last time we talked about him," Rachel said with a sly look. "But please, let's not go into it." She didn't feel comfortable discussing her mother's love life when her own was such a mess.

"Are you happy for me, darling?"

"Of course, Mom. But the important thing is that you're happy."

"Oh, I am."

"Have you set a date?"

"We're going to wait until Molly gets here. Won't she be surprised?"

"*Surprised* is the word for it. By the way, we got a letter from her today. Things have worked out for a new doctor to take over and she's going to be here in time for Christmas."

Lydia hugged Rachel. "Things couldn't be more wonderful."

She wanted to share her mother's happiness and she put up a good front, but inside, Rachel was thinking how much better things could be. She had her work cut out for her if she was ever going to convince Joe that she had the best interests of Morgan's Point at heart.

Both Margolian brothers were pleased with Cypress Knoll after their tour and promised to have an offer ready for Rachel within a few days. She was to drive to their corporate office in Jacksonville on Wednesday to pick up preliminary plans for the project. She would present these to the town council at the regular monthly meeting on Friday.

In the meantime, she mostly sat around the house and brooded. On Saturday she got the urge to clean her mother's house from top to bottom. Maybe that would work off some of her nervous energy.

"You're more depressed than I thought, dear," Lydia said as Rachel rummaged in the utility closet for the mop and broom. "I want you to tell me what's going on with you and Joe. What caused your falling-out?"

Rachel sat on the kitchen floor and explained what had happened. Lydia was quiet as she described her last confrontation with Joe.

"You see," she summarized, "I want to help this town. You need a clinic here and with Molly coming I thought she could be persuaded to stay. Joe is so damned stubborn, he won't listen to reason. All he can see is his own viewpoint. Well, say something, Mom."

"I was just thinking how much you had presumed. You don't even know if Molly will be interested in settling in Morgan's Point."

"If she's not, we'll find someone who is. I've read about the shortage of doctors in rural areas and the kinds of creative arrangements towns have to make to entice them in. A small, but fully equipped clinic would be a very good incentive. The town could agree to deed half interest in the clinic to the doctor if he or she contracts to stay for five years. It's worked for other towns."

"So you're planning to stay here?"

"Well, no. I'll be going back to Jacksonville. I have a business to run, Mom. You know that."

"I love you, dear, and I know your heart's in the right place. But it seems to me that if you're not planning to stay in Morgan's Point, you really have no business trying to tell us what to do."

Her mother's words were gentle, but their impact struck Rachel like a blow. "I'm only trying to help."

"Morgan's Point has gotten along for nearly two hundred years without your help, Rachel."

Rachel got up and stomped into the living room. "You sound just like Joe!"

"Maybe Joe's right."

"You don't even know what plans the Margolians have. They could be wonderful."

"Neither do you, dear. They could be awful."

Lydia's words turned out to be prophetic. The following Wednesday, Rachel sat in a luxurious conference room at the Margolian corporate headquarters as the brothers unfolded their plans for Morgan's Point.

What had Joe called it? *Rape.* It was an apt description of the devastating commercialism the Margolians had in mind. When she tried to explain the historical significance of the area and the importance of preserving as much of the natural beauty as possible, Dan Margolian laughed.

"Florida is full of pine and cypress woods. There's nothing unique about those at Cypress Knoll. As for the animals, I guess they could be relocated before construction begins, but it will have to be at the town's expense."

"You mentioned additional expansion," Rachel said, the sick feeling growing in her stomach. "What would that involve?"

"We want to build a thoroughbred racetrack. It'll bring in business for our motel."

"Motel? I thought it would be a good idea to convert some of the older homes into bed-and-breakfasts for tourist lodging."

"Nah, that wouldn't be economically feasible. We'll get a franchise with one of the big chains. That area out near the old school would be perfect."

"What about the school? It was constructed in the 1800s, you know."

"That explains why it's falling down. We'll put a little marker up where it once stood. That'll satisfy the history nuts."

Rachel felt faint. Hadn't she said those exact same words only a month ago? Had Joe seen her as she was now seeing the Margolian brothers? Savvy businessmen concerned only with the bottom line? Had she really been that thoughtless and selfish?

The answer to all her questions was a resounding yes. No wonder Joe wouldn't speak to her. She didn't want to speak to the men in front of her, but she knew she must.

"I'm sorry, gentlemen. But your plans are not what I expected. It's important for you to be willing to work with the mayor of Morgan's Point and the people to preserve the small-town flavor and integrity of the area. If you won't do that, I'm afraid I can't accept your proposal."

Dan Margolian began rolling up the plans. "I'm sorry, Ms. Fox. But our contract clearly states that we have final word on all construction. It doesn't work to have too many fingers in the pie. We buy the land and then we do what we want. That's my offer. If you don't think you can work with us on this, we'll find another agent who can. I'm sure the right person can persuade the good people of Morgan's Point to see things our way."

Rachel was so hurt and angry, she was trembling. He was right, of course. If she didn't take the offer to the town council, someone less scrupulous would. Someone whose only goal was to make a few bucks and further his career. And the people might go for it. Hadn't she set it all up? They wanted that clinic and they might outvote Joe to get it.

God, she'd made a mess of things. Why hadn't she listened to Joe? Why had she been so stubborn? He wasn't the one who was wrong, she was. She never should have butted into things. Morgan's Point wasn't her town.

She drew herself up in her chair. "I'll be happy to take your proposal to the town council," she said in a flat voice.

"Now you're talking, Rachel. I knew a sharp cookie like you wouldn't let a little sentiment stand in the way of making money."

Rachel sat quietly as Joe presented his plan for Cypress Knoll to the council members. Working with a senator from Florida, he'd managed to get the government's Department of the Interior to commit to leasing the land for one hundred years, if the town approved. Under the plan, the U.S. Forestry Service would be responsible for turning the thousand acres into a national wildlife refuge and managing it for the duration of the lease. The animals would be protected and cared for, the ecology would remain intact.

To enhance public use of the area, the government would construct hiking trails and primitive camping areas that would be supervised by a resident forest ranger. These would pull in tourists year-round and the town would benefit from additional revenue.

He outlined the plan in detail, but not once did he make reference to Rachel's proposal. Not once did he try to influence the council by saying derogatory things about the Margolian brothers. He never even mentioned Sinola.

As Rachel listened, she realized that the income from the lease was nowhere near what the town needed to construct a clinic. She could tell by the looks on the council members' faces that they weren't buying it. She'd won and she hadn't even presented yet. Why didn't that make her happy?

She tried to speak to Joe when he finished his talk, but he brushed past her. At the door, he turned. "I promised I'd present my case and leave it at that. I'm keeping my end of the bargain. At least I still have principles."

That jab was meant for her. "Why didn't you tell them about Sinola?"

"No dirty tactics. Remember?"

The big dope. His principles and integrity had not served him well this time. He turned away from her and disappeared into the night. She knew she'd never see him again.

After Rachel made her presentation, she went straight to her mother's house. It was after ten o'clock, but she'd decided that she couldn't stay in Morgan's Point another hour. She went into her room and started throwing things in her bags.

Lydia came in and sat on the edge of the bed. "What are you doing, young lady?"

"I'm packing."

"I can see that. So, you're running back to Jacksonville with your tail tucked between your legs. I didn't know I'd raised a quitter."

"Mom." So much pain and frustration was packed into that little word.

"I want you to stay."

"I can't. How can I face Joe now? God, Mom, I love him and I didn't even realize it until I saw the look he gave me tonight before he left the meeting. He thinks I betrayed him and he hates me. I can't stay another minute with that hanging between us."

"Then go to him and explain."

"I can't."

"Can't, can't, can't. Is that all you can say? All that means is that you won't. You have just as much stubborn pride as Joe Morgan. Maybe more. The two of you make a fine pair."

"Mom, try to understand."

"I'm sorry, Rachel, but I know you and Joe are in love. I know how good you could be for each other. Why, anybody with one good eye and half a mind can see that. You need to go to Joe and work things out. Compromise.''

''I think Joe loved me once, but he doesn't feel the same way now. He hasn't spoken to me in over a week. His secretary has orders not to admit me to his office. Tonight at the meeting, he let me know exactly what he thinks of me.''

''Go to him. Tell him he was right and you were wrong. Tell him what you told the council tonight.''

Rachel zipped her soft-sided bag. ''No. I won't do that. I guess my stubborn pride won't let me. I have to leave.''

Lydia stepped in front of the door. ''You can't go now.''

''Oh, yes I can.''

''I've got a call in to Molly. She'll be returning it any minute. Don't you want to stay long enough to tell her the good news about the clinic?''

Rachel relented and let her mother have her way one last time. She went into the backyard and sat in her favorite chair to wait in lonely exile.

Mrs. Puddleduck waddled up to her and laid her head in Rachel's lap.

''I never thought I'd need your company, but I'm glad I have one friend left,'' she told the bird.

A mournful ''Quack, quack,'' was her friend's only reply.

''Yeah, that's right. Life's pretty pitiful, isn't it? Tonight I'm driving back in my classy car to my classy house in my classy neighborhood. Bright and early Monday morning I'll be behind my desk in my tasteful, well-appointed office, raking in a tasteless amount of money. Everything a girl could want, right?''

''Quack, quack.''

"You said that already," Rachel pointed out. "A month ago, I would have been thrilled at the prospect of getting out of this little nowhere town. When I came here, it was like I'd been marooned on another planet. I really hated it."

"Quack, quack."

"But now, the thought of leaving makes me miserable. That classy house in Jacksonville doesn't even feel like home anymore. I found that out when I stayed there this week. Dammit, it feels like a hotel and not even a very warm one at that. Go ahead, say it. Quack, quack."

"You know, Puddleduck, I wish my life were as simple as yours. I wish I could waddle around my backyard all day, eat a little corn, lay a few eggs. Pinch the derrieres of people I don't like. What a way to grow old."

The duck looked up as though offering sympathy, and Rachel went on with her monologue.

"I don't want to go back to Jacksonville. I want to get out of the rat race for good. I want to accept that offer to sell my business and stay here and get married. I want to raise my children here and be the grande dame of Morgan's Point."

"Would you settle for being the first lady?" asked a familiar deep voice behind her.

Joe couldn't believe what he'd heard. He'd known Rachel had changed, almost as much as he had. Her actions at the council meeting had proven that.

Rachel jumped up, her sudden movement sending Mrs. Puddleduck squawking away. "Joe! How long have you been hiding there in the dark?"

"I wasn't hiding. I was just waiting for a break in the conversation to announce myself."

"How much of that did you hear?" She was embarrassed and excited at the same time. She didn't really want anyone to know that she talked to ducks, but so long as that person was Joe, she didn't mind too much.

"Just about all."

"What are you doing here?" She didn't really care, she was so damned glad to see him.

"Earl Potts just called me. He told me about your presentation to the council. Why'd you do it, Rachel?" He took her hands in his, eager to touch her, to assure himself that he hadn't lost her after all.

"You were right, Joe. The Margolian brothers wanted to come in here and scalp Morgan's Point. Their plan amounted to developmental looting. I knew I had to present it to the council, though, or they'd just get someone else to."

"Do the Margolian brothers know what kind of picture you painted of them and their operations?" he said with barely concealed amusement.

"No. But it serves them right. They don't deserve to be a part of our town." She slipped her hands from his and wrapped her arms around his neck, pulling him close.

Joe's hands rested on her hips. "Earl said you'd figured out a way for the town to accept my plan and still get the clinic." Although talking was the last thing he wanted to do at the moment, he knew they needed to discuss things.

Rachel's fingers stroked the hair at Joe's nape. "When I was in Jacksonville this week, I talked to a lot of people I know. I got enough pledges from individuals and corporations to start a building fund."

Joe's skin tingled at her touch. "Woman, you're making it very hard for me stand here and discuss business."

The desire in his voice made her feel more wanton than ever before. "It pays to have friends in high places," she said with a grin.

"If push ever comes to shove, I want you on my side."

Suddenly he pulled her to him, and she felt her soft curves press into the unyielding strength of his body. "That doesn't sound like a male chauvinist attitude to me." Her voice was a husky whisper.

"This male chauvinist has had his consciousness raised."

"Among other things," she said with a soft laugh.

"What can I say?" He grinned. "You have an uplifting effect on me." He lowered his head to nibble her ear.

"Don't you want to hear about how we can get matching funds from a government program through the Health, Education, and Welfare Department designed to help establish medical care in rural areas?"

He nibbled some more. "I'm listening."

She sighed. "It's kind of difficult to keep my mind on business."

"Glad to hear it. We're making progress." He massaged her back and pulled her closer.

The sooner she told him, the sooner they could get on to more important matters. "The town can contribute whatever it makes from the Follies and the Autumn Festival and I got a bank to agree to loan the rest."

"Good for you."

"The money we get from the government lease will cover the mortgage payments. And with any luck at all, Molly can be persuaded to stay and practice in Morgan's Point."

"That's nice."

"Are you listening to me?" she demanded playfully.

Joe really did want to hear what Rachel had to say. He just wished she'd tell him later. Much later. But since she was determined to clear the air between them, he would have to wait. He stopped nibbling at her neck and looked deeply into her eyes. "You have the majority of my attention. Tell me how you managed to accomplish so much in such a short time.''

She stroked his face and outlined his lips with her fingertips. ''I'm good at what I do,'' she said slyly.

He kissed her fingertips. ''You can say that again. Did you mean what you said earlier about wanting to sell your business? You don't have to.''

''I want to. I think I've wanted out for a long time—I just didn't realize it.''

''I thought it was more than a livelihood. It was your life.''

''That was before I met you. Before I realized how much I was missing.'' She told him about her wish to write how-to books. ''Besides, I'd still have the Morgan's Point office. Mom wants to retire now that she's getting married.''

''Would that be enough for you?'' he asked, still worried.

''It is now.''

As his friend had pointed out, love could solve all kinds of problems. He and Rachel were living proof. He kissed the tip of her nose. ''Will you answer my question? The suspense is killing me.''

''Which question was that?'' She felt her insides start to melt. God, would Joe always have this effect on her? She certainly hoped so.

''I asked if you could settle for being the first lady of Morgan's Point.''

''What do the duties entail?'' she teased.

''You'll have to appear with the mayor at all town functions,'' he said with mock seriousness.

''Is that all?''

''You'll be required to go to Perkins' Ice Cream Emporium at least once a week and eat a banana split.''

She considered. ''Hmm.''

Relive the romance. . .
Harlequin and Silhouette are proud to present

A program of collections of three complete novels by the most
requested authors with the most requested themes.

Available in February:

It was over so long ago—yet now they're calling,
"Lover, come back!"

Three complete novels in one special collection:

EYE OF THE TIGER by Diana Palmer
THE SHADOW OF TIME by Lisa Jackson
WHATEVER IT TAKES by Patricia Gardner Evans

Available wherever

books are sold.

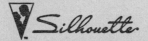

**And now for
something completely different
from Silhouette....**

Unique and innovative stories that take you into the world of paranormal happenings. Look for our special "Spellbound" flash—and get ready for a truly exciting reading experience!

**In February, look for
One Unbelievable Man (SR #993)
by Pat Montana.**

Was he man or myth? Cass Kohlmann's mysterious traveling companion, Michael O'Shea, had her all confused. He'd suddenly appeared, claiming she was his destiny—determined to win her heart. But could levelheaded Cass learn to believe in fairy tales...before her fantasy man disappeared forever?

Don't miss the charming, sexy and utterly mysterious
Michael O'Shea in
ONE UNBELIEVABLE MAN.
Watch for him in February—only from

Silhouette
R O M A N C E™

Don't miss these other titles by favorite author

PEPPER ADAMS!

Silhouette Romance®

#08724	CIMARRON KNIGHT*	$2.25	☐
#08740	CIMARRON GLORY*	$2.25	☐
#08753	CIMARRON REBEL*	$2.25	☐
#08842	THAT OLD BLACK MAGIC	$2.59	☐
#08862	ROOKIE DAD	$2.69	☐
#08897	WAKE UP LITTLE SUSIE	$2.69	☐
#08964	MAD ABOUT MAGGIE	$2.75	

*Cimarron Stories

TOTAL AMOUNT	$
POSTAGE & HANDLING	$
($1.00 for one book, 50¢ for each additional)	
APPLICABLE TAXES**	$_____
TOTAL PAYABLE	$_____
(check or money order—please do not send cash)	

To order, complete this form and send it, along with a check or money order for the total above, payable to Silhouette Books, to: **In the U.S.:** 3010 Walden Avenue, P.O. Box 9077, Buffalo, NY 14269-9077; **In Canada:** P.O. Box 636, Fort Erie, Ontario, L2A 5X3.

Name:_____

Address: _____ City: _____

State/Prov.: _____ Zip/Postal Code: _____

**New York residents remit applicable sales taxes.
  Canadian residents remit applicable GST and provincial taxes.

PABACK2

Silhouette®